I0595326

Charles Edgar Spencer

The Viking Guy

Legend of the Moxahala - and other poems

Charles Edgar Spencer

The Viking Guy
Legend of the Moxahala - and other poems

ISBN/EAN: 9783337391041

Printed in Europe, USA, Canada, Australia, Japan

Cover: Foto ©Andreas Hilbeck / pixelio.de

More available books at **www.hansebooks.com**

GUY,

LEGEND OF THE MOXAHALA,

AND OTHER POEMS.

BY

CHARLES EDGAR SPENCER.

PHILADELPHIA:
J. B. LIPPINCOTT & CO.
1878.

DEDICATION.

TO MY FATHER AND MY MOTHER.

If aught of beauty, truth, lives in my song,—
   Caught from the mystic human heart, the blaze
   Of summer suns, the forest's dreamy ways,
   My life's sad days as swift they ebb along,
Or aught beside in Nature's wondrous throng,—
   Worthy or of remembrance or of praise;
   My love would here transfer the lowly bays
   And twine them on the brows where they belong:
For where my heart is, surely, there should be
   These fragments of my heart, with all their dower;
   Receive them, then, though humble as the flower
And moss of hidden dells; and they, to me,
   Shall thus become a treasure far above
   All price,—the tokens of my love—my love.

CONTENTS.

	PAGE
DEDICATION	3
THE VIKING.	
Advertisement	9
Prologue	13
GUY.	
Part the First	43
Part the Second	72
Part the Third	102
LEGEND OF THE MOXAHALA.	
Preface	133
I. The War-Party	137
II. The Indian-Fighter and his Cabin	143
III. His Youth	151
IV. His Home near Seneca Lake	160
V. The Last Conflict	170
OLELA: A WANDERER'S VISION OF PEACE	179
MISCELLANEOUS POEMS	
Ouranopetes	195
Lincoln: An Ode	203
Soliloquy of One returned to the Scenes of his Childhood	206
An Hour of Slumber	211

PAGE

Hymn to the Ocean . . 212
Summer Days 223
Hymn to the Incomprehensible . . 225
The Aztec Maiden . 227
A Dream . . . 232
Written on the Hudson . 238
The Angel of Song . . . 242
Night . . . 246

SONGS AND BALLADS.

Thistle Seeds 251
Little Nell, the Pride of the School 252
On the Recovery of a Proud yet Beautiful Young Lady. 257
"I Think Aye of Thee" . . . 258
A Picture 260
Hope 265
The Evening Paper . . 266
Song 269
Maid of the Mohawk . . . 271
"Ah, now the Song is Flown" . . . 277
Sir Tristram's Song to Queen Isoude . . 278
A Lover's Love-Ballad . . 281

SONNETS.

On a Deserted Cottage in the Alleghany Mountains . 285
On the Death of Ada 287
On Reading Shelley 288
Adieu to Life, from the German of Körner . . 289
To —— —— 291
On a Favorite Cat named Don Juan . . . 292

NOTES . . . 295

THE VIKING.

" Here is the Quene of Faerie,

  With harpe, and pipe, and simphonie,

    Dwelling in this place."

      CHAUCER'S RIME OF SIRE THOPAS.

7

THIS tale is founded on the old Norse superstition that the cataract of Vöring Foss is haunted by water-spirits, that fascinate those who view the waterfall, and tempt them to leap over the giddy brink. Brace, describing this the most beautiful of all the cataracts of Norway, says:—

"The water comes silent, swift, with hardly a foam, to the ledge and then makes its quick leap of eight hundred and fifty feet into the abyss below; first it is foam, then spray, then beautiful descending wreaths of silvery mist, whose intertwining and changing shapes, quick appearing and vanishing in a thousand fantastic figures, one can watch by the hour, and fancy all manner of witching Norse Nöke and water-spirits. The grandeur is more given by the great depth and the worn walls of mighty rocks below than by the Fall itself. Yet even the depth you do not appreciate till you throw a stone into the chasm, and count by your watch the time of descent. One can understand, in such places, the Norsk superstitions of the Nöke—the water-spirits, who fascinate and tempt in the beholder. The continuous rush of waters, the roar below, the dancing, fascinating mist-wreaths put you into a dream, so that you can hardly force yourself to rise."

Bayard Taylor says of the same waterfall:— "At last, we approached the wreath of whirling spray, and heard the hollow roar of the Vöring Foss. The great chasm yawned before us; another step, and we stood on the brink. I seized the branch of a tough pine sapling as a support and leaned over. My head did not swim; the height was too great for that, the impression too grand and wonderful! The shelf of rock on which I stood projected far out over a gulf one thousand two hundred feet deep, whose opposite side rose in one great escarpment from the bottom to a height of eight hundred feet above my head. On the black wall, wet with eternal spray, was painted a splendid rainbow, forming two-thirds of a circle before it melted into the gloom below."

To those who have visited the waterfall I would say—if I have heaped up mountains in the wrong place or have taken any other poetical liberty with the surroundings—that Poesy *is* a sorceress, and deals with realities as if they were, indeed, " such stuff as dreams are made of;" and, besides, I have seen the Vöring Foss only in imagination.

In regard to the supernaturalism of the following poem it is scarcely necessary to speak, notwithstanding some critics have held that fairy-tales and the like, of whatever kind, are below the dignity of poetry—suitable only to very young children and very credulous old women. This, I think, is unworthy of serious refutation. Is Bürger's Der Wilde Jäger less striking because we have never heard the Wild Huntsman wind his horn and dash away in the demoniac chase? is Homer less sublime and Homeric because we

know his gods and goddesses, with their plots
and councils, are nothing but mere creations of
the brain? is A Midsummer-Night's Dream less
beautiful, as a work of art, because we common-
place mortals are debarred from seeing Puck
apply love-charms to the eyes of sleeping lovers,
and because we never meet with his fairy-peers
darting, like electric sparks,

> "Over hill, over dale,
>> Thorough bush, thorough brier,
>> Over park, over pale,
>> Thorough flood, thorough fire"?

THE VIKING.

PROLOGUE.

O YE! who dealt unto a darkling world
   The dire reward of superstitious sloth,
Whose sinewy arm and fearless spirit hurl'd
   Vile impotence to naught, and sear'd the growth
Of rottenness that canker'd many a land
   (When man had fallen so low that serfs were loth
To leave their serfdom),—Norsemen! still your hand
      hand
   Hath left its mark on nations! Still the earth
Retains your footprints in its shifting sand;
   And still your blood imbues—nor is there dearth
Of your deep-burning ardor to be free—
   A holier fire, a higher moral worth
In races that are noblest. On the sea,
   Where Nature speaks of Freedom, was your
      home!

The storm, that rolls the waves with madding glee,
  The breaker-bar, where heaves the boiling foam,
The blue expanse of Ocean, boundless round,
  Leaving you free at will to rest or roam,—
These are poetic Freedom, and they found
  Embodiment in what ye did, and bore
Upon our destiny.—Ye first descried
  This wrong-named world—our own hesperian
    shore !
Say ! was it not your valor, often tried
  In mortal combat in the days of yore,
That tingled in our veins, and did provide
  A Henry's eloquence, scarce known before,—
A Franklin, sage the reins of state to guide,—
  A Jones to scourge the sea with sword and
    brand,—
  A Washington to found a glorious land ?

I.

It hath been many eventful years
  Since, in the Scandinavian clime,

Brave Uldrick and his hardy peers
   Would list the scald's inspiring rhyme,
And quaff their copious horns of mead,
And boast of scar and warlike deed,
And tell of Odin's blissful shore,
      Where they should fight
      From morn till night,
And wounds should heal and ne'er be sore!
But, though their lusty laugh is still
   And moons have waned and ages fled
And drinking-horns no more they fill,
   Their memory is not wholly dead;
For scalds have oft the story told—
   To chieftains full as brave as he—
Of Uldrick, once a Viking bold,
   When Norsemen sail'd the sea.

II.

Lithe as the reindeer, brawny, tall,
   Was Uldrick with the yellow hair;
In mien and step and voice withal
   He bore the chief's commanding air;

For well he knew his fathers long
  Had been renown'd in many a war,
And that, in tale and victor-song,
'Twas sung their noble veins along
  Had pulsed the blood of mighty Thor.
His sword hung down, a ponderous weight,
  Dangling from his golden belt;—
Ah me! theirs was an adverse fate
  Who e'er its keen destruction felt.
Within his deep-blue eye there burn'd
  A fire that proved him not of those
Who, from emprise, can e'er be turn'd
  By hardships or the fear of foes;
    For, once begun,
    He scorn'd to shun
A danger—so the end be won.
For this his comrades loved him well
  And follow'd where he bravely led;
Full well they knew, whate'er befell,
  They had a Chieftain at their head.

III.

Within a sombre, wild fiord
   The Viking built a dragon fleet
And mann'd it with his pirate horde,
   And all, at length, was made complete.
At sunset, 'mid a deafening cheer,
Through mountains echoing far and near,
He wound his magic ivory horn,
   And gave the long-desired command
That they should sail at early morn
   Toward the merry southern land,
      Where maidens fair
      With hazel hair,
And gold, and wine, should be their share,—
And where the sun shines warm and bright
As in Valhalla's vale of light.

IV.

But Uldrick, stretch'd upon his bed
—His muscular arm beneath his head—

A heavenly vision saw in sleep,
When silence reign'd at midnight deep:
A Lady, radiant as the sun,
　　Embraced and kiss'd him where he lay,
And with her witching beauty won
　　The heart no queen could steal away!
She then besought him not to sail,
　　And bade, instead, that he should cross
O'er mountain wall and mountain dale
　　Till he should come to Vöring' Foss,
And, when the moonlight silver'd all,
To view th' enchanted waterfall.
And when, alas! she did depart
She bore away his valiant heart.

V.

Said Rolf the Seer,—
　　" Why stand'st thou here ?
Hast thou not cruised full many a sea
　　To flowery lands where grows the vine ?

Where women are fair as fair can be ?
Where golden spoils await for thee,
    And brimming casks of Gaulish wine?
What is there in an empty dream
    Though thou shouldst dream it o'er and o'er?
A meteor with a faithless beam,
    A vacant mind, and nothing more.
Thy goodly crafts lie in the bay
    And idly rock in every breeze,
While thou dost speak of vain delay,
    Nor sail'st across the deep-blue seas.
Thou erst didst love the stern-cut shore
    Where rocks uplift their heads on high,—
The giants dire that lived of yore,
    That, turn'd to stone, through murky sky
Scowl downward with the look they wore.—
    Thou erst didst love the maelstrom-whirl
And surf-capp'd breakers' deepening roar
    And white sea-foam's fantastic curl ;—
Such were thy joys in years before !
O ! why thus idly dost thou stand
    And speak of mountains bare and bleak ?

The sea is blue ! the air is bland !
    And Fortune's smile to seek !"

VI.

A week had pass'd, and yet the fleet
    Still rock'd along the shelving sand
Within the harbor's safe retreat,
    That, girdled round on either hand
By lofty mountains, crown'd with snow,
Lay darken'd by their shade below.
And scarce a single sound was heard
    Upon the beach, so lately rife
With jocund shouts and idle word
    And all the din of busy life.
For, save the guards—a trusty few
Still left behind,—the stalwart crew
Had gone with Uldrick far away,
    Although with ill-dissembled grief;
But not a man could disobey
    The mandate of so loved a Chief.
The mountain-towers that loom'd o'erhead
Hung poised more awful, huge, and dread;

The craggy cliff, the dark ravine,
   The far-off wold of blasted pine,
The ghost-like mists which rose between
   The towering peaks from off the brine,
The deep, deep silence—how sublime!—
   Disturb'd but by the sounding wave,
Telling of endless, endless time—
   Not life's short hour before the grave,—
Were more majestic, wild, austere,
      Since on the shore
      Were heard no more
The laugh and song rise loud and clear.
And over all there seem'd a gloom
Prophetic of disastrous doom.

VII.

Brave Uldrick stands at Vöring Foss
   Where sprayey drops, like crystal tears,
Hang shimmering on the shaggy moss
   Which clothed the rocks a thousand years.
The full-orb'd moon is beaming down
   Upon the wild, the glorious scene,—

O'er mountain, rock, and deep ravine,
And o'er the torrent weaves a crown
Of iris tints and mingling sheen
In clouds of spray, that, floating, wreathe
The rocks where thundering waters seethe.
The Sea-king, lost in thought profound,
Stands off a distance from his men.
The deafening, beating, awful sound
Reëchoes back from mount and glen.
And o'er the Chieftain falls a spell,
A strange delight, a nameless power,
That makes him feel that he could dwell
(Nor ever ask a nobler dower)
With Nature, in such grandeur dress'd,
Forgetful—dreaming—bless'd.

VIII.

The wreaths of mist, like sprites, arise
Oft half invisible to the sight,
And, drifting, change their moon-lit dyes—
Now yellowish dun, now silvery bright;

And with how many a shape and size
  They float through floods of lambent light,
Or, in some shadow hanging dim,
Are changed to Jötuns huge and grim!
And as they sink or upward go,
  While breezes waft them here and there,
Some catch a tremulous Tyrian glow
  Like fairy gossamer on the air;
But grander far the lace-like sheets
  Of quivering spray,—the torrent's hiss,
And roar, as down it pours, and beats,
  And whirls—into the dread abyss!
Enrobed in terror, gloom, and night,
  Hemm'd in by rocks that touch the sky,
Wild hell of beauty! fell delight!
  Whose sullen thunders never die!—

IX.

Says Rolf the Seer, whose hoary hair
  Dishevell'd streams upon the gale,—
" No sight so grandly, wildly fair
  Was pictured e'er in song or tale!

'Tis said that on the mist and spray
  The Water-Spirits ride along;
While with fantastic romp and play
    Queer elfin hordes, a wanton throng,
      Swarm shouting after
      With silent laughter,
And blow the clouds-like thistle-seeds,
    And catch their comrades as they fly
Dragging them from their airy steeds,
    Though all unseen by human eye!
But many a scald has whilom told
    How mountain shepherds oft have seen
The Water-Sprites their revels hold
    To crown with mist their lovely Queen,
Who was more fair, in regal state,
    Than are the nymphs with heavenly graces
That, smiling from Valhalla's gate,
    Await their lusty lords' embraces."

x.

O list, that wild, unearthly strain
Now indistinct, now soft and clear!

O list, it comes again, again,
  Falling how sweetly on the ear!
      'Tis touch'd with sadness—
      The soul of joy!
      'Tis heavenly gladness
      Without alloy!
Ha! now the torrent's voice is still—
  The mountain-walls alone repeat
From grot and glen and darksome hill
  The roar that died beneath their feet.
The echoing thunders die away;—
The crags have caught the elfin lay!
To many a mountain's clifted side
The music trembles far and wide;
      'Tis on the air,—
      'Tis everywhere!—
The stars look down with pleased affright;
The night is redolent of delight;
Enchantment waves her mystic hand—
Changing the scene to fairyland!

3*

XI.

Says Rolf the Seer,—" On you we call,
  Ye sisters weird, O guard us now!
Ye Powers of Light in Odin's hall,
  O shield—we bow! we bow!"

XII.

Lo, spray and foam, a pearly shower,
Are made a throne by magic power,
Upon whose curious-sculptured sides
How many a dewdrop glancing glides!
The diamond sparks, with ceaseless motion,
  How quick they fade—to being start,
As oft, at night, o'er summer's ocean
  Bright phosphorescent wavelets dart.
The canopy, how rich and gleaming,
  Festoon'd above without support!
No Indian sultan, lazily dreaming,
  On such a throne e'er held his court.
Ha! on the air strange spirits stand
Holding the throne with many a hand :—

Such jocund pigmies—
Such queer enigmas;
Some with bright tresses, some without;
Some, romping, wing them round about;
Some, flame-like, shimmer
And, fading, glimmer,—
Wild meteors flitting in and out!

XIII.

The pæan-strains how startling sweet
From many a fairy's scallop-shell!
With what voluptuous power replete
Is every tremulous sink and swell!
Now falling sadly;
Now rising madly;
Now ringing gladly;
Now sinking low, low, low, serene—
O list, a silvery voice is singing,
A deep enchantment wildly flinging
Over the scene!

XIV.

SONG OF THE FIRST SPIRIT.

Sprites! arise from 'neath the wave
    Where the sun ne'er sheds his beams,
Where the pearl and beryl pave
    Blossomy leas with mellow gleams,
And the star-like diamonds clear
Flash their radiance—Hear, O hear!

SONG OF THE SECOND SPIRIT.

Sprites, arise! the Queen commands;
    Ouphes and elves, prepare the way;
Bind your locks with misty bands,
    Don your gossamer rich array.
Through the blissful power of love
Comes the Queen to earth above.

SONG OF THE THIRD SPIRIT.

Fair Gunylda, mightiest Queen!
   Leave thy gleaming, crystal halls,
Where the velvet mosses green
   Overdrape the dewy walls;
Come, O come! we wait for thee
Bowing low on bended knee.

SONG OF THE FOURTH SPIRIT.

Rise to earth, O Lady fair!
   Come, eclipse the moon's bright day;
Leave that land whose nectarous air
   Is like spice of Araby,—
Where the waters' lullaby
Murmuring on shall never die.

SONG OF CHORUS OF SPIRITS.

Hail, Gunylda! Queen of Beauty!
    Who is half so fair as thou?
Lo, thou com'st—here we in duty
    Lowly, lowly, lowly bow.
Hail, O Queen! how bless'd is he
Whom thou tak'st thy love to be!

XV.

Says Rolf the Seer (a space apart
    Is Uldrick from his awe-struck men,
Who turn, bewilder'd, with a start
    To hear a *human* voice again),—
"If e'er ye practice Runic spell,
    Now is the time for shielding power;
For ye, who practice Runes, 'tis well—
    This is a dreadful hour.
Beware! beware! the Sprites impel
    Beholders o'er with vile deceit
To leap the falls—a thousand feet,—
    Oh, 'tis a direful hour!"

XVI.

Behold, she mounts her gorgeous throne,
Calm, peerless, beauteous, grand, alone !
  How queenly doth she wear her crown
Blazing with many a radiant gem !
  The mist-like drapery streaming down
Half hides her moon-lit diadem.
Her eyes—no gem was e'er so bright—
  As blue as heaven—bewildering eyes !
More soft than moonbeams' quivering light
  O'er lakes that mirror back the skies.
      Jewel'd with brightness
      Her robe of whiteness,
From graceful neck and breast of snow,
  How stately falls in many a fold
O'er limbs just outlined faint below,
  And form of round, voluptuous mould !
What alabaster could compare
With brow so pure, so pearly fair,
Sunny with wavy golden hair ?

XVII.

Brave Uldrick stands and gazes o'er
　　The awful brink beneath his feet,
　　Down, down, where dashing torrents beat
In but the passing hour before.
　　The dizzy depth is heeded not;
　　The peril dire he hath forgot;
One minute, yea, an instant more
That foot-press'd rock may downward slide—
Ye Powers! the tottering rocks divide,—
　　Ah—now they, turning, catch again.
　　There's naught his mazy senses ken
Of all the danger; naught beside
　　Those smiling eyes upturn'd to him,
　　Whose love-light makes the moonbeams dim.
He speaks in musing undertone:
" The lovely face, the lips of red,
　　How oft I kiss'd them in my dreams—
And waked to find the vision fled!
　　The shower of hair with sunny gleams,

The slender waist with gemmy zone,
    The blue, blue eyes I saw in sleep,
    That seem'd not eyes they were so *deep*,—
Now, now, they shall be all my own!"

XVIII.

O list! she speaks,—a language sweeter
    Than is the Norseman's harsher tongue;
    'Tis smoother than the scalds have sung
Their ballads in mellifluous metre.
Now meet reply does Uldrick make
    (His voice replete with passion's fire
    Thrills like a heavenly-finger'd lyre,)
In language like to that she spake.
    Ah, Uldrick, who has taught to thee
So soft a tongue? ah, why forsake
    The Norse, the fittest for the sea?
He turns with hands upheld in air,
    And lifts him to his fullest height,—
    A towering form against the night;

Over his forehead, broad and bare,
The night-wind toys his dampen'd hair,
    He seems in act to draw and fight;
He leaps!—The foot-press'd rocky ledge
Has fallen prone o'er the yawning edge—
    Down! down! he's lost, he's lost to sight——

XIX.

Says Rolf the Seer,—" My heart hath beat
    A thousand times since Uldrick fell!
    When will the falling fragments tell,
With awful crash, the fate they meet?
    Hark, now the trembling rocks repeat
        The sullen sound they back repel!
    They, thundering, quake beneath my feet.
        A knell—a knell—a doleful knell;
           Oh! let it swell."

XX.

The moon is hid behind a cloud;
    A sudden mist has gloom'd the gale;

The rocks appear amidst the shroud
  Like monsters indistinct and pale.
  The waters, hissing, whirling, roaring,
Raise up their deepening voice aloud—
  Into the deep black caldron pouring.
Unseen they sweep along, and sink
  Plunging through shades of nether night,
Save, just along the darkling brink,
  Glimmers a foamy line of light.
The fairy shells have ceased to ring;
  The vision fled,—so passing strange;
The voices hush'd—no longer sing:
  Ah, joy and beauty ever change.
Still, elfin-like, a witching strain
  Is lingering on the night-wind sighing;
The sweeter sighs alone remain—
  Now e'en the wind itself is dying.
Now, far and near, the torrent's sound
  Among the rocks and caves rejoices,
Echoing wildly round and round—
  A choir of muffled ghostly voices.

XXI.

The cloud is passing—passing—gone,
    The moonlight floods the wonted scene.
The spray and foam whirl on, and on,
    With all their former varied sheen,
And turn and roll in shapeless form,
    As, oft, at summer eve, are seen
The thunder-clouds amidst the storm,
    When genii vile bestride the blast
    Heaving them onward dark and fast.
The beauty, glory, grandeur, fear,
    That fill the scene, crowd on the heart,
Leaving a seal, which many a year
    Shall last,—yea, haply ne'er depart.

XXII.

Says Rolf the Seer,—"Oh welaway!
    What woe is ours, my gallant men,—
We all may live our earthly day
    Nor have so great a Chief again!

The bravest king that sail'd the sea,

With heart like Ocean's, throbbing free.

Woe, woe is ours, my valiant men,

We'll ne'er have such a Chief again!"

XXIII.

Says Rolf the Seer,—" Let Uldrick rest,

The rocks the pillows 'neath his head.

The dashing spray will o'er his breast,—

What recks he, cold and dead?

Through all the long, long winter drear

An icy shroud shall fold him round,

Nor could so grand a place be found

In which to lay our Chieftain dear.

His corse shall hear the pattering sound

Upon his tomb of crystal clear,

When drive the snow, and hail, and sleet,

The drapery o'er his winding-sheet.

And when the winter, cold, severe,

Dissolves his stolid icy chains

And genial summer smiling reigns,

He, resting on, shall ever hear
  The falling waters' awful roar;
'Twould fill some hearts with dread and fear,
  But Uldrick loved the grand of yore:
To him, 'twill be the best of cheer;—
  A foamy pall shall fold him o'er;—
Each drop of spray shall be a tear.
Yon chasm shall be the proudest grave
Where slumber th' ashes of the brave!"

XXIV.

A space, the men all gaze below
  Each with a sad and downcast face,
And turn them slowly round to go,
  To hie them from the fatal place,
    Ruing the day
    They left the bay.
Thus, leave they there their Chief for aye,
  And cross the mountains, crag and moss;
And slow the roaring dies away
  Of wild, majestic Vöring Foss.

*   *   *   *   *   *   *   *

XXV.

We know not what we seem to know,
   Our vision scarce exceeds a span;
We see not what the years shall show;
   We winnow—but retain the bran.
How wondrous is the web of life!
   Delight full often ends in sadness;
Events with keenest sorrow rife
   As often herald joy and gladness.

'Tis said by those who oft have seen
   That, when the moon is full and bright
   And Vöring Foss is robed in light,
Upon a throne of gorgeous sheen
   Brave Uldrick reigns a king beside
The Water-Spirits' beauteous Queen—
   His loved, his fair, his elfin bride.
If this be true, it is not strange
   That—as they tell—he ne'er hath sigh'd
In all these centuries, fraught with change,
   To in Valhalla's bliss abide.

They say he reigns th' immortal king
  Of fair Gunylda's murmuring land,
Where all the year is blooming spring
  With odorous zephyrs breathing bland,
And unseen harps forever ring,
  And princedoms wait at his command;
Where falling founts, with lulling sound,
  Through many an agate palace run;
Where diamond-lamps shed glory round
  Like southern California's sun;
Where shimmering dewdrops ever flow
O'er flowers that never cease to blow.
    Said Rolf the Seer,
    With many a tear,—
" O! may our mighty Chieftain rest!"—
  He knew not that, when Uldrick sprung,
'Twas but to reach the haven-breast
  Round which his arms have ever clung,
    Loving, beloved, and bless'd.

GUY.

Heu, quoties fidem
Mutatosque Deos flebit, et aspera
Nigris æquora ventis
Emirabitur insolens !

HOR., LIB. I. OD. V.

41

GUY.

PART THE FIRST.

THERE are whose lives, from birth oft unto death,
Are shadow'd by misfortune, and, without
Sufficient cause on their own parts, are cursed
With woes and peace-destroying ills beyond
Those who have more deserved them. Such be-
    come,
Through lengthen'd suffering, skeptical at heart—
Losing their faith in virtue and in Heaven.
And, though for them, at last, the clouds *should*
    break,
There ever must remain in such sad souls
A part of their accustom'd gloom; which, nor
The natural goodness of a gifted mind,
Nor all the untold beauty of this world,
Can e'er dispel.—Now be it mine to trace
A portion of th' events of such a life;—

Of one endow'd above vulgarity,
Who, if his birth had been beneath a star
Not unauspicious, had been, haply, great;
But, ruin'd and unhappy as he was,
Is worthy still remembrance—and a tear.

There is a land that breathes of mystery—
A vast extent—the home of solitude
Primeval.   There the long-maned buffalo
Feeds o'er the great savannas, herds of deer
Snuff the free air of taintless purity,
Roaming at will; and, midst the forests dim
And mountain fastnesses, the grizzly bear
And panther have their lair.   It is a region
Whose huge cloud-piercing mountains wind away
In chains of many a hundred miles in length,—
Whose awful torrents and calm-flowing streams
Make Europe's rivers seem as rivulets,—
Whose plains are boundless like the sea.—A land
Of forests, lonely lakes, and deserts drear,
And dread canyons in whose all-voiceless depths
The mighty rivers seem, unto the eye

Dizzy and awe-struck, like diminutive ribbons
Of silvery light;—a land whose myriad spots
Of beauty, quietude, fertility,
Do seem as they were made to be true
Terrestrial paradise.   O what a realm
Is this great West!   What will it be when time
Shall have subdued its vastness by the might
Of cultivation!   Will it not become
The world's rich harvest-field? will not its crops
Feed those that hunger in far-distant climes?—
Yes, if our Country's Liberty survive,
It shall be fair Progression's chosen home.
But if our Freedom perish—O may he
(If one e'er plot to mar—destroy our State)
Be damn'd to live a lingering life, and feel
The conscious baseness, vileness of himself
His upas curse, till withering self-contempt
Consume him!—Ay, if Liberty survive,
It shall become the store-house of the world:
But now it is untenanted, save where
The march of civilization has begemm'd
Its marge with cities populous; and save

The few remaining Indian hordes that rove
Its woods and prairies.   All this Western World
Is yet in infancy.   Its history seems
A day, when thinking of the distant reign
Of Cheops or the city of old Ninus.
What was it in the cycles of the past?
Who were its people ere the Argive bands
Beleaguer'd Ilium?   'Tis a continent
Whose story is conjecture; and the West,
So broad, and lone, and beautiful, and wild,
Is redolent of deeper mystery.

'Twas near the confines of this wilderness,
Upon a morning in the month of May,
When scarce the young leaves trembled 'neath
    the flood
Of golden sunlight, in the gentle breeze
That stole from banks of flowers with scarce a
    whisper,
A Youth, a pilgrim from the busy world,
Stood all alone within a forest dell.
He felt the west-wind ripple through his hair

As warm and balmy as the breath of Venus;
He drank the still enchantment of the scene,
And felt the power of beauty crowd upon
Him and intoxicate with strange delight;
And, feeling e'en as one return'd at length
From foreign lands to home and those he loves
(O blissful moment!), cried—" Here will I dwell,
And ne'er again turn to the haunts of Man—
More lonely than the wilderness!   Ah, yes,
If there is aught of peace, for *me*, on earth,
'Tis here with Nature, whom I take to be
The ever-charming mistress of my heart."

His years were few, and yet his life had grown
Almost a burden; for the magic light,
Which once had fondly seem'd to fill the world,
Had vanish'd year by year until to him
Remain'd but barrenness; and with the change
Himself had changed, till e'en the thrill of joy
Was full of sadness.   Thus, he oft had been
Most sick at heart amid the jarring throb
And noise and bustle of the world, where men

Grow cold and selfish, and had stood alone
Within the crowded mart on gala-days
And at the banquet, rout, and giddy ball,
Longing for something *better* than to live.
Oft in such moments, making them more sad
(Like half-remember'd dreams of happiness),
A spell fell o'er him ; and he heard the low
Soft whispers of the forest and the lull
Of dimpling waters and the song of birds,
And saw the far blue sky, lone hill and dell—
Fair Nature's varied face with all its smiles
And nameless beauties,—and he caught the breath
Of violets and wild-roses and sweet thyme
By limpid brooklets where the humble-bees
Are ever busy ;—and he deem'd 'twas well
That he should leave the throng and wander far,
As others thought, in solitude, but where
For him there was society, and dwell
Alone with Nature and his sadden'd heart.

For he remember'd how in earlier youth
He oft had walk'd with Nature.   Even then

The spirits of the universe had stoop'd
To be his high companions, and the winds
Were his wild playmates, and e'en trifles were
To him as friends, and charmed beauty grew
A wondrous mirror that did half reveal
The mysteries of eternity and truth.
Nor was it thus alone in time of flowers,
And birds, and sunshine.   When the southing
     sun,
At Capricorn, turn'd toward the gusty North,
The snow, that fell so spotless o'er the fields
And lonely wood and hamlet,—clouds, which
     lower'd
In gloomy grandeur,—yea, the howl and dash
And tumult of the tempest, that recall'd
With sadden'd pleasure summer's stilly days,
When night had fallen and all without was dark
And drear and dreadful!—and the deep, deep
     blue
Of heaven, when winds were still and midnight
     clouds
Were scatter'd, seemly groundwork for the stars

(The hieroglyphics of that grandest vault),—

And moon, that smiled enchantment o'er the

　　　earth ;—

These were most eloquent, and waked in him

The deep unspoken poesy of the heart,

E'en as the wanton winds, in sunny June,

Dancing on tip-toe o'er the nodding fields

Of sweet red clover.

　　　　　　　　In those happy days,

He loved the mountains, climbing at his will

Their steep and shaggy sides e'en to the clouds

That mantled o'er their summits.　By the sea,

The ever-rolling melancholy sea,

He loiter'd oft to watch the dark wild waves

And list the music of their dissonance,—

The mightiest minstrels of the earth.　And thou,

Sublime Niagara ! how swell'd his heart

When first he saw thee through thy misty veil,

Crown'd with thy rainbow-diadem !　He watch'd,

Rapt with the grandeur of the scene, for hours,

Thy beauteous deep-green waters rush amain,

Dappled with patches of fantastic froth,

On to the awful gulf—and, thundering, die,
Stunn'd at the bottom in wild-curdled foam!
And, musing on thy driving spray, he saw
How mutable, how short is life, beside
Th' eternity of Nature; and he felt
The impulse of idolatry,—he scarce
Refrain'd to leap into thy turmoil—lose
Himself in *thee*, O Irresistible!
Lodging within some cottage near thy brink,
Full oft he thought, half-dreaming, through the
      night,
He heard the hoarse tornado, then awoke
And listen'd to thy jarring sullen roar,
Rising and falling with the midnight gale,
Sounding forever.—
          Oft, when others stood
Aghast, he was most happy.   'Midst the storm
He seem'd the Genius of the elements.
The boding breathless hush,—the darkling clouds,
Heaving against the sky, o'ercapp'd with light
Like Ocean's wrecking waves,—the sudden stir
Of trembling leaves upturn'd,—the playful leap

Of blinding lightning,—the bough-rending storm,
And deepening roll of thunders, making earth
And air to palpitate,—the tear-like drops,
Large and pellucid, pattering here and there,
Prelusive to the pouring of the rain,—
Then the dim wall of drops innumerable,
Continual falling, shutting from the eye
The humid landscape;—such were his delights.

In field and wold, fann'd by the cool free air,
There was for him a never-ceasing pleasure.
The willow, drooping pensively as fill'd
With his enduring sadness—stately oak,
Patrician of the forest—sighing pine
With scented shade and soft wild melody—
And linden, with its air of cheerfulness,
Waving its blossoms to the breath of June,
Are all endow'd with an intelligence
That waked an echo-sympathy in his heart.
Thus, through the many animate forms of life;
He held them all as kindred.   Savage beasts
He saw, in fierceness, are not unlike men.

Loving to trace through all those lower lives
The glimmering light of reason, he had mark'd
The war-horse, prancing, snuff the air whene'er
Sounded the rolling drum and bugle-blast,—
The faithful dog go many a weary mile
Home to his master, poor howe'er he be,
And there with eloquent gestures of delight
Express his joy and undissembling love.
These taught him how presumptuous are the minds
Tumid with what they deem profoundest lore,
That fancy all the mighty universe
Was made for them, for their poor sovereignty,—
Self-constituted puppets of low pride—
Earth's demigods of rapine and conceit!
Such he would leave and feel himself to hold
A nobler station in the scale of things,
That he, in humbleness, could hail all life,
All Nature as his kindred and his friends.
And thus it was that he became, as 'twere,
Companion of the universe, and made
High friendship with the soul of solitude,
Speaking a language that is not of speech.

And, studying that most aged, truthful page
Outspread before him, pondering deep and long,
He learn'd what all the schools could teach him
    not.

But he did turn from Nature to abide
With Man, though in his heart there were most sad
Misgivings—though he sigh'd to be again
Wafted along the deep-blue lake and free
Among the mountains.　He did turn away
From that which was his joy unto his woe.
Bright dreams, the ignes-fatui of the brain,
Oft haunted him and pictured to his mind
Most sweet and heavenly things,—that he might be
A benefactor, blessing to mankind;
For he was fill'd with love for all the world
And noble aspirations to do good.
Thus, with a heart susceptible of deep
Delight and love, despair and misery,
He turn'd to tasks by him not understood,
And, ah! how ill-requited.　What a change
The earth would show, if each but knew himself—

For what he is most suited!   Still, methinks,
There would be many a hapless son of earth
So born beneath the shadow of mischance,
And nurtured up, without his fault, to be
A child of sorrow, that, e'en then, this life
Would oft be dark, unhappy.   Thus, with him,
Whate'er he nobly did for others' weal
Reverted on himself in bitterness.

He had full many friends whom he did trust,
Deeming them truthful as himself: and one,
Who shared his joys and griefs, his highest hopes
And dearest aspirations, whom he loved
E'en as a brother.   But, alas! how few,
That cloak them under friendship's holy name,
Have other love than their own selfishness—
Are else than parasites of prosperity,
Envying most the one they call their friend!
Those who profess'd to him the greatest zeal,
Ever in honey'd phrase, did secretly
Revile him; and the one, whom he loved best,
Treated him most ungratefully when fortune

Ceased smiling for a moment.   Pitying them,
He cast them off in sore disgust at man's
So abject perfidy.   Henceforth he came
To doubt mankind; and even in himself
He lost his wonted confidence.   He trusted
None, ever after, that did call him *friend.*

There was a maiden younger than himself,
Whom, e'en in schooldays, he was wont to view
With boyish admiration; in whose face
He scarcely dared to look for bashfulness—
Yet, whose bright smile he fancied was as sweet
As his own mother's.   Her he help'd to cross
The icy places on the way to school,
On winter mornings, carrying oft her books
Right gallantly; then, haply, all the day
Felt happy, though he knew not why, and conn'd
His irksome tasks with something of delight.
But this was all the joy he had at school,—
He was a strange, wild being, loving most
To wander through the fields and ancient woods,

And study what he pleased by fits and starts,
Hating the dull routine day after day.

Then there were years in which he saw not oft
This maiden ; but, whene'er they met, there seem'd
Some new-born beauty, charm in her fair face,—
Some added grace of person; and her voice
Grew softer still and sweeter.   Even then
He look'd into her eyes with strange pleased awe
Because of their shy loveliness ; and all
Her girlish ways, ridiculous in themselves,
Commanded, for her sake, his due respect.—
Yea, that which had been silly in another,
In her, became a beauty to his eye.
Yes, he had loved her, though he knew it not,
E'en in the blush of girlhood ; and his heart,
When she had grown to womanhood, adored
With all the passionate ardor of his youth.

His mind, which, in itself, had long become
A golden treasury of most lovely truths
And images of beauty, gave to her

The halo of its lustre with each thought,

As brooklets seem to tinge with their own hue

The pebbles white seen through them.   Dreaming
        dreams,

Sweet in their unreality, he made

Her empress of a bright ideal world,

Created all for her.   He fill'd her being

With spiritous love and loveliness beyond,

Yet, meet to one so fair and fairy-like,

And braided for her brow a wreath of all

Or bright or beautiful, until he came

To love an earthless soul divine, that dwelt

Only within his dreams—the heavenly birth

Of his own fancy,—that in all the world

Had not existence.—But he knew it not,

Nor dream'd that she was less than he had dream'd.

And, gazing in her soft and luminous eyes,

That ne'er reproved, he drank the wine of love,

Deep draughts of blinding love, until, for him,

There was nor joy nor bliss—save in her smile.

He would have given his dearest hope in life,

Drunk with the 'wildering ecstasy of love,

To fold his arms, beneath her streaming hair,
About her waist—kissing her loving lips!—

Meekly coquettish, she would smile, half frown,
And smile,—and lead him on with those coy arts
That seem so artless; acts, which, of themselves,
Are nothing, but to him who madly loved
Were priceless,—El Dorados of the heart.
But they were all deceits to hold the sway
The longer o'er her vassal (to enthrall
With the dull torture of uncertainty),
Evading ever; for with secret pride
She knew he loved her, and she felt too well
It was an honor to have gain'd his love.
Yes, she was but a woman; and her heart—
Like others of her sex—could learn to love
The tinsel glitter of some puny Crœsus,
Won by his servile haughtiness, yet turn
From him, who, as a plain and honest man,
Dares whisper the devotion of deep love.

Alas! alas! there is no sadder sight
In this wide world, that is too often sad,

Than, having built an idol to adore,
To see it fall from its exalted niche
E'en while we do it homage, and to know
'Tis earthy as the dust wherein it lies.

When he perceived the baseness of the mind
Which he had thought to have been ever fill'd
With love and beauty, stunn'd, he fled away,
Dizzy with vague bewildering woe, which changed
Gradually to th' acute despair of his
Wild nature.   Often he essay'd to laugh
Fiercely and like a madman at his pain;
But, while a ghastly smile o'erblanch'd his cheek,
His heart was wrung with deeper agony.
He did upbraid her not, nor saw her more:
But the last look of disappointed love,
The silent eloquence of his sad dark eye,
Did leave a withering poison in her soul;
Which, suddenly, when she else had been most
          happy,
Stifled the thrill of joy, and made her feel
The damning pang of lingering self-contempt.

He did upbraid her not, nor saw her more;
And, fleeing like some criminal, hunted down
With echoing hue-and-cry, he fled the scenes
Of home and youth, most dear, and cursed himself
That he could love one so unworthy love.
But he, methinks, could not but still adore
That Beauteous One who dwelt within his dreams,
Round whom he had entwined so many thoughts
Of beauty and sweet purity divine
And heavenly high affection, though he knew
'Twas but a radiant phantasm of his own
Creation—an ideal of a soul,
Without an earthly likeness.
      O how hard
He strove to tear that sorrow from his heart—
That morbid woe that crush'd him with its weight!
As, in the desert of the far Southwest,
The stunted tree, beside the dried-up fount,
Droops through the rainless season of the year,
'Neath the fierce fiery sun, until the leaves
Are parch'd and crisped; even so, he felt
His heart consume its own vitality—

Withering in utter loneliness.   The few
That would have loved him truly to the last
Had died before him.   Weeping o'er their graves
He long'd to be a sharer in their rest,
And, in his frenzy, raised his lawless hand
To smite himself; but some distracting thought
(The chance that moulds how many an earthly
       act)
O'erbridged the moment that had been his death,
And he survived to suffer:—such is life.

Ambition, oft the last dark solace left
To genius fallen in sad degeneracy,
Had lost for him the stimulus of excitement;
For, e'en in brighter days when he had hoped
To be successful, 'twas not for himself,
But those who loved him; and he knew there beat
No heart that loved him in the wide, wide world.—
O earth! thou art a dark and dreary waste
When there are none to love us—none to love!
For life becomes, in its sterility,
A winter without hope of coming spring.

He thought to lose remembrance of himself,
Of that which *had* been, and what *might* have been,
In sin's dark-whirling maelstrom.   Driving on
Before the passionate storm within his soul,
He ran from vice to vice without a care—
Without a fear; as some ill-fated bark,
Driven before the unrelenting gale,
Flies to its ruin.   Soon he learn'd to laugh
In mock derision at all sacred things;
And sainted virtue he did call a name—
A thing without existence save in thought.
Full many a gray-hair'd wanderer from the right
Beheld, with wondering awe, himself outdone
By that apostate Youth, e'en in the path
Of darkness he had follow'd all his days.
For noble minds, though warp'd and sadly fallen,
Proclaim their high supremacy above
The shoals of mediocrity, and wear
The laurels—though in Pandemonium.
O what a change! O what a dreadful change
In that young Spirit!   Once, that soul had been
The dwelling-place of beauty, the abode

Of something like to heaven;—now grown, alas!
The fell and darksome prison of itself.—

How quickly sin doth dull the sense of right!—
He judged from her, the Lady of his love,
That women aye are sirens,—that *all* smile
Or to mislead or catch a golden moth.
Th' ingenuous face, the shyly half-raised eyes
Of innocent girls, he deem'd to be the arts
By which he suffer'd; and he look'd again
Upon them with the blighting evil-eye.
To him they were deceivers all, at heart,
Whom it were well in justice to deceive;
For, sure, deception is a game at which
It is not meet that *one* should play alone.
His voice was most mellifluous, like sweet rhyme;
Its accents seem'd the language of true love;
And he could whisper in a lady's ear,
Though 'twere dissimulation, that sweet tale
As long as she could listen—too well pleased:
And his impassion'd eye—O, 'twas not well,
When it did speak a language sweeter still,

To feel its glances; for it was enough
To have seduced a more angelic being.

Thus he descended to a sensual world
Of libertines and wassailers, who mock'd,
Over their wine, the peace they ne'er possess'd.
But ever—in the midst of pleasure—dwelt
With him the haunting knowledge, that, if *this*
Were truly *life*, 'twere better to be dead—
Ay! never born; and that the universe
Were all a mighty failure, worthy naught
But to be wreck'd and dash'd to utter chaos.

There ne'er is such impenetrable night
But, somewhere, from the earth a star is seen:
There scarcely is a sorrow so intense
But hope may glimmer through it: and, methinks,
There is no heart so vile that it retains
No lingering virtue.   Though he had become
A libertine, whose pallid cheek reveal'd
His wild excess, that Youth was still at heart
A seeming contradiction,—evil mix'd

With much redeeming goodness. He had found
The vices, which had seem'd Lethean draughts,
Possess'd no opiate powers, but that they left
Deep in his soul the rankling of remorse.
And he perceived, what he had long in vain
Endeavor'd to disprove unto himself,
That virtue still were virtue, though mankind
Were wholly sunk in baseness and in crime.
In double wretchedness he lost desire
To live; he long'd for any change of state,
E'en though it should be to acuter pain,
From that benumbing agony of being.
In those dark hours he look'd around upon
The things which, in his childhood, had been
    loved,
Remembering all the careless happiness
Of those far halcyon days; but they invoked
Deep-thrilling sadness—bitter, bitter tears!
The magic of existence—the tried charm,
Which maketh pleasing e'en unpleasing things—
Had perish'd: the elixir of the soul,
Transmuting every feeling at its touch

To something bless'd or beautiful, was gone,
And would return to him—ah! nevermore.

But, with these melancholy thoughts, there came
The recollection of the beauteous forms
Of Nature, interwoven with his youth,
And the delight they erst had given him.
And, holding in his hand a goblet brimming
With wine, he saw a forest-spring and heard
The hurrying tinkle of its pearly stream,
Plunging o'er mossy rocks, beneath the heads
Of yellow crowfoot, pale anemones,—
And in the dream, he dash'd away the glass:
Then, bowing low his face upon his hands,
He gave him up to fancy.—
                  He beheld,
In panoramic beauty, many scenes
That once had been familiar (as the young
Enthusiast erst had seen them), with a part
Of the enrapturing pleasure he had felt.
The far snow-crown'd Sierras loom'd again
'Midst their salubrious atmosphere: the sea

Of prairie-grass and flowers, unbounded round

Save by the sky's pure azure, waved beneath

The scented gale: again, he sail'd at peace

Over the sea-like lakes, and floated down

Majestic rivers: and he pitch'd his tent

Beneath the dusk pine-forests of the West,

And heard the soul-felt music of their leaves;

And, round his camp-fire, sat, in reticence,

The black-hair'd Indians, in whose belts were seen

The tomahawk, and knife, and dangling scalp.

The picturesque wild aspect of these scenes

Changed to full many a simpler home-like spot,

That he was wont to love,—to hills and dells,

Dotted with peasants' cottages, where streams

Wound on in gentleness—beneath the boughs

Of overhanging woods,—as blue as heaven.

Awaking from that bless'd forgetfulness,

How terrible was the quick-returning sense

Of anguish !—He would seek those happier scenes—

Fly from the feverish world! which aye to him

Had been so dark a dream. In solitude,

Dwelling afar, he deem'd that he might find
A soothing balm,—perchance, a fount of hope.

And, thus, a willing exile, he became
An eremite, an outcast from the world ;
And, on that morning of the youthful year,
He cast him down upon a mossy slope,
Beneath the gnarled aged trees.   It was
A spot of wondrous beauty, lone and wild,
Amid the primitive wilderness.   Long time
Before, while journeying through the West, he
        chanced
To spy the hidden loveliness of the place ;
Long, long it haunted him in memory—
Its spirit of peace : and now, at length, most sick
Of life and, oh, how weary ! he had come
To dwell amidst its solitude.
                    A change
Already stole upon him.   Seemingly
He felt new animation in his blood,
Caught from the life around ; his sunken cheek
Was tinted faintly with the hue of health ;

And his dark eyes, that still were wont to speak
So eloquently ere his voice could fall
In sweetness on the ear, burn'd with a fire
More hopeful than their former languid light.
Feeling the undertone of sympathy
That wells from Nature to the heeding heart,
He dream'd he would not there be all alone
Among so many lives,—the only friends
That ne'er would be unworthy of his love.
Yes, he could call them friends; for, musing there,
He dream'd that all, all life shall be immortal
If there is immortality for man.—
Does not the lowest, shortest life, too, flow
From the same fountain of all life, and light,
And motion?   What is this fell monster, Death?
Who knows ?—There was, somehow, a mystic
       voice
In the green leaves above, and in the flowers
And fairy fields of moss on which he lay,
And birds that sung so sweetly overhead,
That told his heart, convincingly, they were
All children of one mighty family,

And he was but their brother.   Then he dream'd
That, after he should pass that portal dim
(If death does open to a future world),
He there should, haply, some time see a bower
Like to the life of that in which he lay,
And, stretch'd upon the violets, there behold
The leaves wave o'er him in the gentle air.—

PART THE SECOND.

It was a scene of quiet loveliness,—
A varied landscape, broken here and there
In spots of rugged beauty, but more oft
Navell'd with shadowy dells and hidden nooks,
In whose sequester'd grottoes gentle echo,
Mocking the song of bird and babbling stream,
Murmur'd a drowsy melody more sweet
Than e'er were numbers of Sicilian pipes.
A woody range of circumambient hills,
Whose bases lapp'd with ever new effect,
Sloped to the waters of a crystal lake
Sleeping a tremulous crescent at their feet.
But not a herd grazed on the hills, nor bell
E'er broke their stillness. Following up the stream
Falling a bright cascade into the lake,
The nearest grange was situate leagues away
Hard by a thriving border settlement,

Built on a railway that had pierced thus far
To bear away the lumber of the woods.
Without the pale of man's drear influence,
Here dwelt the Hermit Guy.   His hermitage,
A cottage 'neath a clump of scattering oaks
Upon the upland, overlook'd below
An open prospect ;—fields, whose grassy growth
Was nature's primitive verdure,—many a cluster
Of towering trees, that, standing far apart,
Seem'd squads of giant knights, the foremost guard
Of the great forest which, on either side,
Stretch'd far unbroken,—and, beyond the lake,
The mountainous hills, whose bluish extreme tops
Amalgamated with the distant sky.

Here he had dwelt a twelvemonth since that day
When, fleeing from himself and all the world,
He sought a dwelling in the wilderness.
He found the quiet he had wish'd, for few
Broke in upon his solitude.   He roved
Where'er he listed o'er romantic hills
And through the winding valleys of the woods,

And oft, for weeks, beheld but Nature's face
And heard no voice save hers.   But, thrice, along
The margin of the lake, he heard afar
Some hunter's hounds that, yelping, followed up
The tawny fox;—soon did their baying die
In hollow echoes 'neath th' o'erbrowing hills,
Passing away as quickly as it came.
And, once, in autumn, when the covey'd quails
Were calling mournfully, what time the grouse,
Drumming beneath the sumach-thickets—red
With crimson crops of berries,—jarr'd the air
As 'twere with sullen thunder, or whirl'd up
Whirring, how startlingly, upon the wing;
He met a sportsman from the distant town
With bag of game, and pointer at his heels;
But he nor spoke nor heeded him, and turn'd
Coldly away, as did Napoleon,
Upon his prison-isle, from those he met.
The huntsman, o'er his shoulder looking back,
Went on as one might go who half believes
A spectre near him.   Twice, perchance, beside
There came a peasant searching through the woods

For straying cattle,—going as he came,
A bird of passage.   Thus had pass'd the year.

The only human voice which Guy had heard
Was his old servant Allan's.   Silent, strange
Was this gray-headed man, who, following there,
Became another hermit.   Having loved
His Master well in far more happy days,
He linger'd with him in adversity
Loving him still; for he had been, as 'twere,
The foot-ball butt of fortune in his youth,
Seeing and suffering much and learning little
Save that it was his fate :—thus, he beheld
A sort of higher self in this sad Youth,
And look'd upon him with a reverent awe.
He knew his duty well, nor did he wait
Nor ask instruction; very seldom seen,
He spake not often, for he heeded well
His Master's whim of silent loneliness.
Possessing in proportion to his mind
The power to dwell within himself and be
His own companion, he was not, in truth,

Unlike his Master, who, if he but chose,
Scorning mankind, could feed upon his thoughts—
However sad,—and be not *all* without
A nameless pleasure in unhappiness.

As in the exquisite texture of his mind
This Youth was different from all common men,
E'en so he differ'd from all who have borne
The name of hermit.   Sensitive tenderness,
Not often equall'd in a loving child,
Was ever present in his heart, although
He outwardly appeared to casual eyes
A spirit fierce, and gloomy, and morose.
The flowers of brook-fed leas and twilight woods,
In their frail beauty, spirituality,
Did make him love them.—Thus it was he brought
Unto his cottage mental luxuries,
For which how few had cared or even thought
If cursed, like him, with hopelessness in life.
He fill'd full many a shelf, in his lone home,
With volumes of encyclopedian lore,
Whose fount exhaustless was forever sweet,

Refreshing,—leaving in his wearied mind

A calmness in its sadness, as the sun,

Shining athwart the tempest, 'midst the gloom

Enweaves the rainbow.   He was not alone.—

The spirits of the mighty dead arose

Mysteriously from pages old, and held

Their choicest converse with him ; and he grew

Familiar with the men whose deeds have thrown

Glory o'er man.   O, it is great to leave

A book—a noble, truthful book—behind ;

Which, though the form be dust in kindred
      dust,

Shall ne'er grow old,—an immortality

Of friendship with the wise and great to be.—

Yes, he did love th' immortal fires of song,

Whose heartfelt numbers mirror up to view

The soul's recesses—teaching us ourselves.

His cottage walls were garnish'd with a few

Most beauteous pictures ; and, within a niche

Of logs unhewn in his quaint library, stood

One form, an undraped Hebe, how instinct

With soul—superlative loveliness divine !

And he could wake soft music sweet, which fill'd
His heart with rapture—and his eyes with tears.

A year had pass'd.   More than accorded with
So short a period, he was changed ; for time
Had set a lasting seal upon his form.
Some live scarce half th' allotted time of life,
And die not younger than the hoariest men :
Their lives are swifter, for they feel more deeply
The wear of pleasure—anguish—joy—despair ;
Their minds consume their bodies.   Finest oils
Are most inflammable, and soonest burn—
Returning to their elements.   For, what
Is the true index of our lives ?—the mind
That suffers and enjoys.   Ay, he was older—
But still that canker was within his heart,
Like fell malarial winds, in flowery climes,
Which might have been a paradise on earth,
Poisoning with their brooding pestilence—
Making the spot a desert.
      I have thought,
Musing upon the millions sweeping on

From birth to death,—the herds that do not
    think,—
Who cannot realize the mystery,
The beauty, sorrow, evil of this world,—
That 'tis a blessing to be one among
The thoughtless, never cursed with gazing up
At the bright Unattainable. For, sure,
They are more happy. They do set their hearts
On drossy trifles, and do think of things
Easy to comprehend, and laugh when there
Is naught to laugh at; when they weep, they feel
Not scathing anguish, for their minds are duller;
And, like the skin-clad savage, they care not
O'ermuch for future or dim past, and eat
And drink, and sleep, and toil, and die.—Their lives,
Like sluggish streams, flow calmly on with scarce
A murmur.
        Genius is exceeding thought,
And oft makes miserable the few that feel
Its power within them; their wild passions have
A Titan's might; their love is ocean-like,
Boundless and deep; and tenderness of heart

Is ever theirs.   They see the glory of
The universe, yet feel how terrible
Are life's disasters, and its sorrows dread,—
Love riven by death, the sphinx-like riddle, death.
Their lives are like swift-flowing mountain rivers
That dash o'er horrid dizzy brinks, and whirl
Down beautiful in sprayey splendor.   Though
The sun doth crown them with his rainbow-hues,
Below are chasms where midnight darkness reigns,
And waters seethe in torment and in strife.

Whether he sail'd along the sky-blue lake,
The snowy bellying canvas of his boat
Catching the summer gale,—or, if he walk'd,
At morn or eve or brightly-beaming noon,
Over the fields, or through the whispering woods
Where peace doth seem to dwell,—or, if, at night,
He stood beneath the stars or sad-faced moon
Or tempest rushing swift along the sky;—
He aye was haunted by the demon—thought.
If he could have but lived like those who pass
Existence in the senses, not the soul,

Enjoying thoughtlessly, or those who, in

Their narrow-mindedness, are wont to deem

The petty actions of their little lives

Sufficient to fill up their being; he

Had been more happy: but these were denied,

And he, in true superiority,

Was miserable.   As one deform'd oft feels

A strange desire to gaze upon a glass

To view his own deformity, he felt

A fascination, which he could not break,

Constraining him to ever brood upon

His sadden'd lot.   Where there were none to
        hear

Save the tall trees, the mossy-mantled rocks,

The streams, the flowers, the birds, the restless
        airs,

His long-familiar friends, he spake his thoughts

And fancies freely.   He was wont to roam

In waywardness, unheeding where he went,

Free as the winds, to hold deep converse with

The scenes around about him.   These few scraps,

His meditations and wild colloquies

(But when and where 'twere wearying to relate),
May serve to show the tenor of his thoughts.

"It is not strange the peerless Lancelot
Was fabled to have dwelt, in youth, with her
The beauteous lady of th' enchanted lake;
For fable intertwines the lovely forms
Of Nature with the stories of her knights,
And with their beauty tempts us to believe;—
And what is lovelier than a forest lake?
Ah me! if beauty still possess'd the power
To make me happy, floating, as I float
Upon this almost waveless lake, beneath
The dreamy shadows of the trees that stretch
Their leafy branches far o'erhead, methinks
I could not be but happy!   But a mind,
Corroded with the darkness of itself,
Colors all visual objects with the hue
Of its own fancies, making them, as 'twere,
A mirror to reflect its wretchedness.—
Fathoms below the surface o'er the sand
And rocks and shells and pebbles black and white

The fish glance in the sunlight momently   -
Like meteors through the water: far beyond
Yon bosky promontory, sails unscared
The wild swan, snowy as the clouds that sail
Along the sky: ha! now the osiers green
Are shaken on the shore; the antler'd deer
Bends down its graceful glossy neck to drink—
Now bounds away; the air is redolent
Of melody, and quietude, and peace:
But I agree not with the scene,—the sole
Dark blot upon its brightness and repose!

" Yes, even now, the charm of beauty weighs
Upon my senses stiflingly, like odors
From dewy tropic flowers. The sun-bright hills,
Stretching in many a winding ridge along
Yon quiet valley till the wreathed oaks
That crown their distant summits are resolved
To clouds of dusky azure;—yonder stream,
Plunging with wild tumultuous melody
Into the lake,—the glittering Minnehaha
Of this sequester'd vale,—forever singing

The same sweet laughing song that Nature taught;

The warm June sunshine, streaming over all,

And photographing, on the lake, the form

Of leaf and bough above; *these* and the thousand

All-nameless charms that, intermingling, blend,

Forming the whole, are all how beautiful—

How beautiful!

           " Alas! my soul accords

Not with the scene!—The sweet-breath'd wild-rose

        hangs

Over the rocky ledges of the shore,

Drooping so low the wavelets almost kiss

The pendent leaves ; and, o'er the roses, drone

The honey-laden bees continuously,

Like spirits winging through Elysian vales.

Hark, through the last year's leaves, 'neath yonder

        elms,

The graceful chipmunks, screaming, run at play

In frolicsome delight; they feel the joy

Of thoughtless, free existence—blessed beings!

I would not rob them of their gladsomeness

E'en though 'twould make me happy.—O thou sky!

How canst thou bend so placidly above,

As if beneath thy sapphire-arched dome

There were no crime, no misery, and no death,—

Nothing less pure than *thou?*   To me, the sun

Is virtually extinguish'd, for his beams

Serve only to make visible the gloom—

The shadow o'er my soul.   The loveliness

Of Nature breathes but sadness: Hope, sweet
      Hope—

Where is she? that she smiles not for mine eyes."

*   *   *   *   *   *   *   *   *

" How obvious—how mysterious is life!

To thoughtlessness it is not wonderful ;

But unto him who pries into its depths

It ever grows more complicate and dark,

Until—as he were gazing on the sun—

The light at first beheld becomes a blot,

And he is struck with blindness.   Is there one

Who, searching in th' recesses of his heart,

Finds he is not a stranger to himself?—

Man knows not whence he came, nor where nor
      what

Shall be his destination.   Through a world
He knows as little of as of himself,
He journeys toward a beetling precipice
Wrapp'd in eternal night; and when he falls—
What is his fate?   Alas, the sagest sage
Can tell you what you know—that he is dead.
Ay, death is still inexplicable death ;
The same dull, stifling, chilly torpor dread,
That, when the earth was in her infancy,
Fell o'er the good, the beautiful, the brave,
The old, the young, the infamous, the wretched,—
Freezing alike the blood within their veins,
And leaving to the broken-hearted ones,
Weeping around the bier, a lifeless thing
Men call a corse, which, though too well beloved,
Gives with each icy kiss of its set lips
A thrill of nameless horror.—Who, to-day,
Knows more than this of death's dim mystery?
They, who have laid some loved-one in the grave,
Know only, in their woe, that mother Earth
Reclaims her children all again to be
Hid in the bosom that did nourish them.

"The flowers arise in their allotted times,

And bud, and bloom, and perish.   Here, methinks,

I catch the delicate fragrance of the lilies

Now blossoming 'neath the sunshine on the lake;

Ah! fragile is their snowy loveliness—

Few days will pass ere they will float no more

Upon the water.   'Midst the sea of air

Their soft delicious odors will be lost;

And, save to those who chanced to learn to love

Their saint-like beauty, Nature still will seem

Without a void,—as if no life had fled—

Gone out forever.   Why arise the trees,

Leafy, and tall, and venerable with moss—

Great canopies of shade,—except to die?

They mark their ultimate doom in their sear leaves,

When, driven before the killing autumn blast,

They strew the woodland and the sad-voiced
      brook.

The animals of land and sea and air,

So full of life, so wonderful in form

And mechanism of being, all are doom'd

To the same destiny,—to live, then be

No more: and man, great Nature's sovereign, *man*

Is favor'd not beyond the very herds

That he is wont to call his slaves;—'tis well.

The world is one eternal, mighty death-bed,

Where beings revel in their winding-sheets

And reck not for their ghastliness.   Strange—

    strange—

We all are in a feverish delirium,

Dancing with Death.   In but the passing moment

How many a million lives have ceased to be!

" I dwell full often in a land of dreams.

The twilight of the senses shrouds me from

The visible world; and, drifting from myself,

I seem to wander in th' ethereal realms

Of those departed.   Round about me float

The souls of those I love, and on the air

Are voiceless whispers that are not of earth—

Breathing the burden of enduring love.

Soon, soon, the harsh reality intrudes.

Awaking, then, I know that I have been

'Mongst unsubstantial shadows, airy dreams,

And forms that be not, born within a brain
Throbbing and healthless.

           " At the dead of night,
Have I not studied oft th' dark-woven spells
Of sorceress and magician, on the air
Casting their hellish potency of charms,
Demanding from the dismal silent tomb
One single soul ?   The only answering voice
Was the weird night-wind moaning o'er the roof
Amid the darkness.   Madden'd with despair,
I cursed th' inexorable fiends of hell,
Daring them from their fell abodes (as if
There were such beings), that I might converse
E'en with a demon.   But they came not forth.—
'Neath Hesperus pale, at twilight, I have stood
In peaceful dells' embower'd solitudes,
While in my heart there was a deep, deep woe—
A longing all insatiable, and felt
That, if the ones who loved me once so well
Lived in a higher, better world than this,
They would return to comfort me.   Alas !
The twilight deepen'd into night; I still,

Still felt the same sad aching in my heart.
Ah me! I would that I could be again
Th' unquestioning, loving, all-believing child
That listen'd, while my mother told me erst,
How we at length should go unto a land
Where all the year is beauteous as the May:
Yes, I remember once when I did ask
If, in that bright, delightful world afar,
The sweet pink apple-blossoms ever die,
And if the robins ever cease their singing
And building in the trees;—a tear bedimm'd
Her eyes, as, kissing me, she whispered—*no*."

* * * * * * * * *

" How slowly drag the hours away! It seems
E'en thrice a day since morn o'erblanch'd the hills,
Ashy, and dun, and dull, with settling fogs
And misty drizzling rain; yet 'twill be long
Ere lonelier night, when I may lay me down
Upon a sleepless couch. Chill is the gale
And comfortless, for summer; o'er the ground
The smoke-like vapors creep; and rivulets wind

Over the oozy sod, soak'd to o'erflowing.

Still does it rain, rain on in drizzly gloom ;

The drops wind down the window-panes like tears.

Would 'twere a tempest with hoarse-raving winds,

Thunder, and driving clouds, and lightning dread,

Like the bright sword of some fierce sky-god,
   shiver'd

To glittering fragments high in heaven ! ah, then,

My soul were calmer.   But this housing dank—

I may not plod o'er leagues of wold and hill

To wear me to submission, and my mind

Doth dwell on what it should not.   All day long

The dreariness without, within my heart,

Hath found an echo; for my thoughts have been

'Mongst parted hopes, the ruins of a life,

And misspent days, where not a blossom sheds

Soft fragrance 'mid the dust and ashes.   Yet,

It is not strange I thus turn back in thought,

For I, in youth, believed the world to be

Not what it is.   To know the patriarch,

With saintly beard and longest prayer, to be

The veriest cheat of all who learn to cheat

And call it business; that, in this young land,

The statesman's service is to steal, and damn

Fair Freedom with his name as did Barère;

That virtue sells for gold, and gold doth buy

All righteousness; that sordid, pitiful pride,

Proud not of mind, but chance of birth or place,

May flaunt and flourish, while true worth and
       genius

Despair; that friendship, even sacred love

Are falsehoods, gilded playthings of an hour

For godless hands;—yea, 'tis not strange that one

Learning these things should ponder deep, and
       long

Remember.   Yet, I would forget—would lose

Myself in contemplation of the forms

Of Nature round me.   When th' unclouded sun

Shall beam again on earth, and gentle airs

Fondle the flowers, and cheerfulness and joy

Seem everywhere; I shall forget the past

In the Lethean beauty of the world,

And feel the leafy pleasure of the woods,

And catch a kindred quiet from the calm

Of many a clear Bandusia where the birds

Descend to lave among the sedge and flowers."—

*   *   *   *   *   *   *   *   *

" I had been dreaming of my childhood's home,

Its hallow'd memories, and its well-known haunts,

And of the ones I loved so long ago.

Its days came back to me more sweet because

Of indistinctness; cross-bows, balls, and games

Of hide-and-seek—a medley strange; I grew

Oblivious of the present.   Though I knew

'Twas but a fancy, then, methought, I felt

The presence of my sister—dead long since—

My earliest playmate.   All inaudibly,

Save that I *inly* heard, she sung to me

A 'wildering melody of wild sad airs,

My thoughts according ever with the strains—

Their import pictured in mellifluent tones.

She led me and I follow'd, drifting on

Upon the mazy ecstasies of song.

O! how delicious were the soft sweet strains

That whisper'd of the truth, belief, and joy,

The loving words and actions of those days!
And, O! how like the laughter of a child,
Thrill'd with delight, arose the music, trembling
With transport, telling of the sports and romps
Of long, long summer days, of Maying walks,
And hopes and fancies changing like the wind!
But, ah! how heavenly sad the closing strains,
Reminding me the loved-ones of my home,
My father, mother, she, and all, are dead—
Are dead! and I alone—O God! *alone.*"

*   *   *   *   *   *   *   *   *

" How silent, save the rippling, rustling leaves!
'Tis midnight, and the moon is not in heaven;
But through the clouds that sail along the sky—
Great winged monsters,—many a star looks down
Now calmly from above.   Ye golden Fires!
For whom do your exhaustless lamps gleam on
Eternally?   Not for this atom Earth,
Nor all our little system: I may gaze
In homage on your beauty, but ye know
Not that I live.   Our Sun, that unto us

Is blinding in his radiance, ye, most near,

May see dim as the Pleiads; but this world,

Lighted with borrow'd gleams, dark as the hearts

That dwell upon it, ye may never know

Is in existence.   Yet ye ever burn

On in undying glory, bright as if

Ye were the gods that some have deem'd you.—

  Ye

Seem sown upon the sapphire pave of heaven

So thickly that your gleaming locks might catch

In tangled brightness; but ye stand apart

Immeasurably distant: even thus

Our senses still mislead us.   Thou! dim band,

Thou milky baldric of the universe!

Can we, who have resolved thy nebulous suns

To systems e'en outnumbering the sands

Of Ocean's shore, can we know aught of thee

Beyond conjecture?   Thus, we ever sink

Whelm'd in a sea of vague perplexity,

Finding that all we know but teaches us

That we know nothing.

   "Hark! the answering owls

Hoot gloomily amid the echoing woods.—
The clouds high overhead now fuse themselves
In one unbroken blackness, from the dark
Horizon to the zenith; and the winds,
Arising in their might, uplift a voice
How like the rush of waters; now the rain
Comes on with footsteps pattering o'er the leaves;
And, westward, sheets of radiance fitfully
Illume the heavens, like northern lights.—Ha! now,
The storm-winds grasp the mighty oaks, and writhe
With them in conflict!   Let the shatter'd boughs
Crush me to earth! sick—sick am I of life.
O Storm! thou wilt dissolve thyself in tears,
Leaving the azure heavens again to be
Peopled with stars, and traversed by the moon
In changeful beauty,—but within my heart
The tempest ne'er shall pass away on earth!"

*   *   *   *   *   *   *   *   *

The Summer waned, and melancholy Fall
Stain'd the doom'd leaves with his first touch of
    gold.

It was a morn of this most lovely time:
The air was soft as May, but fitful gusts
Blew unexpectedly among the leaves
With sighs foreboding, and, in sun-tann'd fields,
Bow'd down the heads of yellow-tufted grass
And bore the thistle's downy seeds aloft,
Which, rising—vanishing incessantly,
Symboll'd the ebbing moments of our lives.
The mellow sunlight nestled lovingly
O'er hill and valley and the tremulous tops
Of the far-stretching forest, save when clouds,
Snowy and shapeless, floating on through heaven,
Cast many a moving oasis of shade,
With weird effect, amidst the golden light
Flooding the earth below.

      Within the calm
Of the primeval woods, whose vaulted roof
Admitted 'tween the yet unfallen leaves
But scattering stars of sunshine, which did serve
Only to make more dim its column'd vistas;
The Hermit Guy, with slow uncertain steps,
Follow'd the winding labyrinths of a vale

Toward the still lake below.   A hurrying rill,
Almost unseen beneath the velvet moss,
Danced like a child, and murmur'd at his feet;
But he nor heard nor saw it: flocks of birds
Were chirping in the grapevines overhead,
Picking the purpling clusters, and around
The last of all the wild-flowers of the year—
The pale-blue asters, well-nam'd forest stars,—
Were blooming, soon to die; but he pass'd on
Unconscious of their presence.   His wan face—
O how 'twas changed! a haggard, weary look
Hung on his bloodless lips, and in his eyes
A tearless agony—a hopeless woe.
As fierce, contending armies' trampling feet
Crush out the life of grass and tender flower
In their fell havoc; thus, within his heart,
The warring powers of his own soul had trampled
The flowers of peace, and truth, and love, and hope,
Making his life a desert.

     As he went
He mutter'd brokenly, " Relentless God!
'Tis well that thou dost make but few to feel

This depth of suffering,—this all-crushing knowl-
  edge
Of life's reality,—this last despair
Of peace, of rest,—this lingering death in life !
Leaving the future not a *single* hope—
No smiling phantom yet to lure—lure on
Into its dreary, awful void !——"
                                His brain
Whirl'd with bewildering dizziness ; the air
Grew suffocating ; greenish vapory clouds
Shut out the light of day :—he, staggering, fell
Swooning upon the mossy-robed ground.

But there was one who, in his wretchedness,
Forsook him not ; who, sorrowing, mark'd the
  change
In his pale face, and follow'd him that morn
Feeling a strange presentiment of his doom.—
Old gray-hair'd Allan dash'd upon his brow
The clear cool water of that forest rill,
And smooth'd the locks back from his pulseless
  temples,

Calling his name, until the blood again
Came rushing from his heart, and o'er his frame
There crept a sudden tremor, and his eyes
Lifted their lids; then Allan raised him up,
Tenderly as a father might a son,
And bore him homeward through the woods and
      fields.

When the dull stupor of the swoon had pass'd,
His mind was crazed; he, waking, dream'd; his
      brain
Became a whirlpool of confused thoughts,
Creating in its wild imaginings
A bodiless world of joy and harrowing woe.
The forms we deem substantial were to him
Impalpable.   He dwelt no more on earth.
He fancied, sometimes, he had died and pass'd
To hell's dim second circle; that in which
Francesca, driven before the blackening winds
That ever rage along th' abyss obscure,
Still hangs upon the once delicious lips
Which damn'd her soul forever with a kiss.

" Ah me! ah me! shall I forever hear

These souls forlorn complaining of their fate?

These hopeless cries, O God! these piteous moans!

Freeze me and damn me with their agony

More—more than my own misery.   Alas,

Why am I here?—O thou abhorred shape,

With whom I whirl through this tempestuous air,

I know thee not.   Say, were thine eyes and cheeks

Fairer on earth, that they could tempt the lust

Of a seducer?   Here e'en thy embrace

Doth thrill me not.—Oh! would that I were deaf—

Deaf to this woe, this surging sea of tears!

O man! what homage dost thou owe to Him

Who damn'd thee in thy birth?   The whole crea-
        tion

Is one grand inquisition, poor, poor worm!

Where thou art tortured by the Hand that made
        thee."—

PART THE THIRD.

'Twas midnight; 'twas the wayward, stormy March.

Around the cottage dash'd the furious winds,

Rapping the lattice with a ghostly sound

And moaning on in dismal semitones

Most mournfully.   Oft, for a time, the oaks

And elms, that interlock'd above the roof,

Would vacillate in the tempest with a roar

Like the confused, wild voices of a host

Of demons, while their branches in the night

Did grasp each other; then, perchance, again

Would fall a startling stillness, which would weigh

Upon the heart with vague suspense and make

Each moment seem an hour; until, at length,

The hail and sleet would dash o'er pane and roof

Pursued again by all th' awakening winds.

'Twas such a night as those in which we feel,

In sympathy with the storm that is without,

A shiver to pass o'er us, though not cold;

For, pondering on the past, which is a dream,

And unknown future, which shall be a dream,

And on the present,—then a sea of thought

Comes o'er us that doth make our hearts as sad,

As gloomy as the night; and we behold,

As 'twere, the many homeless ones exposed

To the all-pitiless tempest.

                     But, within

That cottage, brightly burn'd the fire, whose embers

Did wink, and roll, and glow, like Argus-eyes;

And from the ceiling hung a lamp whose blaze

Shed cheerful radiance.   It was silent there

Save from the tumult of the storm without.

Gazing within the embers of the fire

That seem'd to change in keeping with his

           thoughts,

Old Allan sat in meditation lost.

With forehead resting on her hand, whose shade

Made half-obscure her features, there was one

Whose face was pensive, pale, yet beautiful.

Who could she be, that thus had come afar

To this strange dwelling?   In the lamplight
　　　streaming

Upon her half-bow'd form, her yellow locks

Hung o'er her shoulders even to her waist

Like some rich, glittering mantle.

　　　　　　　　　　　　　She arose

And, passing gracefully with noiseless steps,

Approach'd a bed that stood within the room,

And, drawing back the curtains, let the light

Upon it fall.   Emaciated, wan,

There lay a sleeper,—yes, 'twas Guy. She smooth'd

With delicate touches, from his pallid brow

The damp dark hair; and, bending low, she mark'd

That he slept calmly.   Would he wake again,

As he had done so long, unto a world

Of phantasy?   Would his dark eyes again

Look on the friends that minister'd to him,

And know them not? Ah me! that horrible look,

As if the soul had left its tenement—

Would that return, and, brooding o'er the face

Long wont to be the mirror of deep thought,

Dissolve the heart to pity ?   Days before
A change had come upon him ; he had sunk
As with a deadlier illness.   As he sleeps
He hangs upon the verge of death.   At length,
Perhaps, the end has come ; and he, who dared
To search into the mysteries of the tomb,
Must now   succumb   to   Death—all-conquering
        Death.

The Lady gazed upon him as he slept :
Anon hot tear-drops gather'd in her eyes
Dimming her sight, as silently they fell.
She brush'd them from her hastily, and turn'd
To draw the curtains back, when suddenly
She saw his face o'erflush, and he awoke.
Arising on his arm whose wasted strength
Would scarce support him, he look'd wonderingly
At her who stood before him.   She perceived
That he was conscious, that his soul again
Look'd out from eyes not wild, expressionless.
" Where am I ?—who are you ?—O Genevieve !—
Yes !   I remember in that dreadful dream

An angel of all beauty oft did stoop
Down from a better world to comfort me—
Yes—yes—O yes, 'tis Genevieve!"

                              She turn'd
And would have fled, but he did motion her
To draw more near: "Stay or I die"—he gasp'd,
Sinking again exhausted on the couch
In utter helplessness.

                              Beside the bed,
Sobbing, she kneel'd, and whisper'd in his ear:
"O Guy! forgive me that I dared to come.
I did intend to leave ere you should know—
I knew not you would thus awake."—

                              He gazed
Steadfastly in her eyes: "If you forgive me—
Me, who have cast a blight upon your life,
Stay till I die or know that I shall live."

Again she whisper'd something in his ear;
And then with voice just audible she said,
"Think not of me,—my lot has not been all,
All misery." And then she bade him rest,

Placing a soothing cordial to his lips,
Promising she would stay; and soon again
He slumber'd peacefully.   Then Genevieve
Bade Allan leave her there to stay with him;
And, when he had departed from the room,
She, sitting with her head bow'd on her hand,
Wept through the long, lone watches of the night.

Alas! how many thoughts that are most sad—
Misgivings, recollections,—like dim ghosts,
Haunt one who wears the lingering hours away
Watching beside the bed where death may come
At any moment.   Then the loves and joys,
That are remember'd to have been most sweet,
In long-pass'd days of happiness, appear
A mockery; the heart, grown chill with dread,
Appreciates the instability
Of life, love, beauty, pleasure, strength, fame,—all
Life's petty hopes and selfishness.   It seems
A wonder, then, that, when we quaff the cup
Of mirth and sensual pleasure, thoughts do not
Intrude e'en with th' intoxicating draught

Dashing its sweets with gall. What pledge hath man

For one poor moment's bliss beyond that which

He is enjoying?   Daily doth the sun

Arise and set; his coming and departure

By repetition seem a certainty,

Losing their strangeness: yet, more common far

Is life's drear wreck of hopes; for every day

Crushes and withers even to the death

How many!—leaving them without remorse

Among the ruins of the past.   To-day,

We revel, laugh, are gay; to-morrow, weep

O'er one whose life we would have died to save.

We follow still the rising-sun of Hope,

Like one who, gazing on some distant scene

That charms the sight, walks backward through a
　　　　place

Of many pitfalls.   Stop! perchance thy feet

Are on the awful edge.—A day, an hour

May plunge thee in the terrors of despair.

Thinking such dismal thoughts, and of the past

Of her own life, she wept full oft until

The hazy dimness of that morn of March
Lighted again the mist-o'erclouded earth.
But when the eyes of that pale sleeper oped
And still they spake with reason's light, she smiled
As if there were no sadness in her heart,
And sweet—her voice was, ah! how low and sweet,
Seeming the voice of happiness.

How much
The tender touches of a woman's hand
Can smooth the front of sickness!   Like the stir
Of warm, caressing winds among sweet flowers,
Are her all-nameless kindnesses: the dew,
Falling upon the thirsty flowers at eve,
Is like her sympathy: her soul-felt words,
Expressing much beyond what they express,
Fall like a balm upon a suffering spirit.

Days pass'd: and, slowly, scarce perceptibly,
He, who was poised so imminent near to death
A breath had turn'd the balance, gain'd again
In strength.   Days pass'd: and that strange horrid
        hue,

As if th' infectious monarch of the tomb
Had breathed a blight upon his cheeks, became
A less appalling pallor; power to speak
Sweetly as was his wont return'd with new
Desire of converse.   Then they, who had been
The willing slaves to him in his sore need,
Told of his sufferings in the previous months.
Allan related how in early fall
That dreadful malady of the mind had settled
Over his life; how through the winter long
He did commune with strange phantasmal forms—
Inhabitants of lands which were but dreams;
How he declined upon th' approach of spring,
Sinking until he seem'd to stand within
The threshold of the grave.   And Guy replied
That long ere frenzy seized upon his brain
He was aware of his impending doom.
As by the lurid clouds that roll malign
The traveller knows ere long the hot simoon
Will come descending terrible; e'en so,
He saw the tempest that was gathering o'er
To scathe him with its might.   Could he compose

His thoughts to peace?—as easy might his voice
Quiet the turbid deep.
                    The while they spake,
Leaning upon the window, Genevieve
Look'd out as if across the brown bare fields,
For tears she wish'd to hide were on her cheeks;
And, standing there, she humm'd as to herself
A cheerful air to prove she was not weeping.

Then they were silent all, each seeming loth
To break the stillness.   Musing on his life's
So strange vicissitudes, Guy traced it out,
In thought, from cloudless infancy unto
The moment it had grown a blank,—from joy,
And peace, and beauty, till it was o'erwhelm'd
And lost within the maelstrom of despair.
But now did not the hallow'd light of love
Beam on his soul?   Did not love's cynosure,
At which bright Hope might light her lamp anew,
Arise in heaven?   Ay! there were two great
        hearts,
Such as he deem'd were not in all the world,

That truly loved him; rising from their trial
Of pure affection, o'er his path they shed
Benignest influence sweet: yet—yet, for him,
There was an end in life.

                        The twilight dim
Gather'd within the room till they no more
Could see each other's faces, ere a word
Disturb'd that charmed silence.   But, at length,
When through the evening hours on diverse themes
They held choice converse, blending with his
       voice
There was a something new, as 'twere, a magic,
That made the listeners happy ere aware.

Delightful—how delightful is the Spring!
The scarce-heard rustle of her airy garments,
Which are the leaves, and flowers, and tender
       grass,—
The thousand voices that from every brake
Breathe welcome, echoing on the golden air,—
Are all exuberant with voluptuous music.

The realization of a hope deferr'd
Is her long-wish'd-for coming; her warm breath,
The fragrance of her tresses, and sweet smile,
Are like an houri's of the seventh heaven.

When changeful days—in which Dame Nature knows not
If 'tis mild Spring or Winter drear—are pass'd;
The service-berry in the lonely woods
Outspreads its snow of blossoms; then, ere long,
The yellow violet, and the wind-flower white,
And small spring-beauty, pied with stripes of pink,
Rise through the leaves amidst the forest bare,
While o'er their heads the maple's tasselly blooms
Crimson the twigs.   When clumps of thorny plum
In sunny dells burst into flower, and pink
Crab-apple blooms shed fragrance sweet—how sweet!
The delicate leaflets shoot from every spray.
Soon dogwood flowers are in the woods, where birds

Sing in wild concert; and each verdant lea
Is shower'd with gold—a myriad dandelions.

How brightly shines the sun! the blush of youth
Suffuses once again the aged earth;
A new-born splendor, as if some deep spell
Of magian had commanded from the realm
Of Mab her fairy light, glows over all
Awakening Nature.   Blue—unclouded blue!
Is all the sky; which, as in childhood erst,
Looks down upon a world of joy, romance.
Ah me! the murmur of the unheard brook,
The search for bright-eyed flowers, the pleasant
         shade,
The hum of wild-bees, grass so rich and green,
Invite us to the woods and fields until
The heart is sick with longing!   E'en to one
Whose hopes are like the crisped autumn leaves,
The May, with all its million lives that start,
As 'twere a new creation, into being,
Is full of dreamy melancholy joy—
Delicious sadness.

'Gainst that cottage wall

There stood an open portico, which look'd

Far southward over many a lovely scene.

Beneath its rough-hewn roof the zephyrs soft

Did love to linger through the long May-days,

Sweet from the odorous honeysuckles wild

That overhung the shrubs about the door.

Around its unbark'd, mossy columns clung

Virginia creepers, whose embowering leaves

Hung darksome, casting o'er the seats below

A secrecy of shade.   Aloft, the trees

Spread their fantastic boughs, whose foliage

    breathed

Idyls divine of Dryad-melody,

And, waving ever, made the sunbeams dance

Like bodiless spirits o'er the grassy ground.

O, there 'twas sweet on such calm, dream-like

    days

To loiter hours away, to list the thrush

Warble his wild incessant notes, and, faint,

To catch the turtle-dove's low mournful call

Among the distant trees.

                              There, often, Guy
Would sit, scarce able yet to wander far;
And, sometimes, Genevieve would read to him
Some tale of gentle deeds, of ladies fair
And gallant knights and tournaments of old,
Or, bard sublime, whose soul-subduing rhyme
Charms the rapt heart like Ocean's wild sad music.
O what a spell the witchery of a voice
Melting and sweet and heavenly, casts upon
The burden of a song!   As pearly mist,
Glowing a haloey glory round the moon,
Adds to her beauty; thus, doth such a voice
Cast round a song the halo of its cadence.

Beneath that wind-stirr'd canopy of vines
Sat Guy, one morn, while yet the dewdrops hung
Upon each leaf and flower in that cool spot.
"Ah! would that I were other than myself,
That I might think not!   Newly does the earth
Bask in an atmosphere of gladness, peace,
Song, beauty; spring-time's gentle airs—they
      seem

The flutterings of the unseen wings of spirits,
Whose pinions bear the scents of Paradise ;
The very knowledge that the spring is brief,
That winter swiftly comes, now is not sad ;
Earth's mask'd like heaven : but I am not of those
Who may be happy.   O how sweetly sing
A thousand songsters! some have just arrived
Weary with journeying from the warmer South,
Some have endured the rigor of this clime,—
But they do reck not for the past.   That storms,
Hoary with driven snow, have bleach'd and wreck'd
Their last-year's nests, they care not ; they enjoy
The present, nor bethink them of the past,
The future.   List, the woodpecker's drum-like
        roll—
The cawing crows: those sounds to me, long since,
Were O how welcome!   They no more awake
Delight,—they speak not to a sinless soul.
Ah, well, to every heart save mine the May
Is joyous—hope's own month ; its brightness fills
        me
With melancholy strange.   My days are autumn

And change not, save they swiftly bear me on
To a drear winter that will never end.
My heart is dark—O God! have I not sworn
To crush these thoughts? to bar them from my
    mind?
To be myself—myself?   Have I no will?
Must I be driven by thought's impetuous habit
On, on, forever on,—a storm-toss'd bark
Without a rudder?   No; it shall not be.
The world is not what I have dream'd it is—
It may be made the dwelling-place of peace;
'Tis bright and beauteous; 'tis my eyes diseased
That mar its light with darkness.   Man is not
What I have vainly deem'd him: O how much
I've been myself the dupe of my own self!
Wearing my cap and bells, like other fools,
Unconsciously.   Are there not two that love—
That love unselfishly? one deeply wrong'd?
Yes, there are *some* 'mong men who are at heart
Not villains; some most noble, but how few!
Yet, being few, they are more truly precious.

"I will not think; I'll not be sad again;
'Tis most ungrateful thus to overcloud
The sunshine of pure love in other hearts.
Has she not pray'd, whose love is mine, all mine,
That I should cast away this sadness? gloom?
Alas! what priceless treasures I have miss'd—
How much of that which had been bliss to me
By giving joy to others, I have lost
By being thus unhappy.   But a tree,
Canker'd and blasted, bears not goodly fruit:
A heart inured to care and lengthen'd woe
Becomes as bitter as its nourishment,
And may not change to sweetness.   Can I quaff
A purer than my dreggy cup of life?
Ah, no! the past is with me; terrible, dark,
Mysterious, dream-like void!   I cannot shake
Its shackles from me.   Still its awful spirit
Returns and broods, by seasons, o'er my soul,
Till, like the poor, despised old king, I cry,
O let me not be mad! not mad—not mad."—

With airy footsteps, like the prairie fawn's,
Came one beneath the shrubbery of the yard

To where he sat, dreaming of his strange fate.
A moment gazed she on him silently, .
While morning's incense-airs, enfolding her,
Rippled her garments and long glittering hair.

"Ah Guy! why are you sad? I——" "Genevieve!
Forgive me.   Now I am not sad, my love;
The mists of morn are scatter'd when the sun
Looks down from heaven; the sunlight of your eyes
Dispels the twilight that oft gathers o'er me.
O I would ever hear your soothing voice—
Would look into your face and feel the light,
The love-light of your eyes! then I should be
Unhappy never.   O my Genevieve,
I would that I might kiss you thus—thus—thus!
Beneath your streaming hair, o'er lips, eyes, cheeks,
More oft than there are several stars in heaven;
Might clasp you ever, ever in my arms
Thus closely, closely! feel your beating heart,
Your quick sweet breath, your cheek 'gainst mine,
        yea, all
This yielding form to thrill me, thrill me through,

With an electric current of deep warmth—
A tempest of the bliss of love!   My soul,
How beauteous is the crimson of your cheek
Flushing and fading !   Ah ! my wind-blown lily !
Drooping and sinking thus upon my breast,
How much I love you !   Heavenly beautiful
Were those bright eyes when I could look in
        them—
How blue ! now, hidden 'neath their long-lash'd lids,
They are more lovely that they are conceal'd ;
Ha ! now, that they do shyly open—look
Up at me, that again I drink their lustre,
They are a thousand times more fair than ever !

" Ah, yes, I would forever be empaled
By the bless'd bondage of this snowy arm
From all less heavenly.   Is your love, like mine,
Pure, deep, divine, eternal ?   Read these kisses
I shower in ardor on your lips—a language
Deeper than words,—and tell me from your heart.
Ah, can you whisper but a single yes ?
But, 'tis enough ; for, O how much, how much

There is in that word yes—one syllable, yes!
I might say yes and others might say yes,
Yet all be nothing; but when you do breathe it,
It is an oath more worthy of belief
Than the most solemn oath of all the world.
O wrap me in that love, O be my shield,
Supporting though supported, my own life—
Light—only love!   Aye let your soul flow out
And fill me with itself, as now I breathe—
Live in the throbbing heaven of thy embrace!"

Lock'd in each other's arms, long time they were
Thrill'd with the sea-like ecstasy of love,
And spake no word.   'Twas silent all around,
Save many a bird was singing and the boughs
Breathed their leaf-melody.

                   At length, in tones
Sweet with the spirit of his love, he spoke:
" I do bethink me now of one I knew
Long since, who seem'd to animate the earth
With beauty, glory, love, and cast o'er all
The hue of fairy visions.   Long, how long,

I dream'd ere waking.   In those days my heart

Well'd with emotions, wild, impetuous,

Yet pure as mountain springs that gush a fount

Of liquid crystal.   Well do I remember

We stood one eve beneath th' unclouded sky,

And watch'd the myriad stars to die aloft

As the calm moon walk'd up the verge of heaven.

I see her now o'erhalo'd by the light,

The mystery of the moon : I hear again

The sweet, sweet lies she spoke, and I believed.

That night, as home I went, this crime-cursed world

Was bright and pure and joyous; I forgot

'Tis full of evil.   Scarcely did the earth

Make one diurnal round ere I did know

That she was false—false as the meteor wan

Which lures but to destruction.   Then the world

Grew dark, the sphere of sorrow, crime, and death ;

And I forgot all that is better in it.

Thus I became what you beheld me first,

And I have suffer'd.—

                 " But I loved her not

As I adore you now, O my own life—

Not as I love you now, my more than love—
My teacher of forgiveness, lasting truth !
Ah ! why did fate not crush *me*, only *me*,
With all—redeeming you from such deep woe ?"

As on the nerves of smell the exquisite scents
Of dewy hay-fields fall, so on the ear
Fell her sweet, gentle voice when thus she spoke,
Though tears, hot, bitter tears, were in her eyes :
" In every life there are some dark, dark days
That it is well forever to forget.
O let us rather think of happier times
Than—— If I, homeless, loved you still the same,
Was true to you (and, by that Spirit Divine,
Palpable on the very air we breathe,
I swear it), what do matter all my trials ?
You said you loved me : 'twas not wholly false,
Else why should it have proven true at last ?
The past be past : its sorrows—leave them with
The lifeless hopes, the vain regrets, that haunt
Its Stygian darkness.　Only one dread day
Will I recall, for on that day there broke

A light from heaven.   I knew not that you lived,

Till he, the best of all mankind save you,—

Most noble Allan,—bade me journey here

To see you die.   I came—to see you live;

O my beloved! like these enfolding arms,

Let present bliss surround us and shut out

The past; and, wedded as we now are wed

By love's enduring compact, let us think

Of that which *may* be, not of what *hath* been,—

Of happiness through love,—of infinite worlds,

Through whose progression love shall lead us on—

Most blessed star!—to the ne'er-coming end."

*   *   *   *   *   *   *   *   *

The sun had set; the stars look'd dimly down;

Like courses of blue rock far to the west,

Loom'd up the cloudy battlements of the sky;

And pure as tears of joy that hang suspended

Upon the lashes of a woman's eye,

A million dewdrops on the tall, cool grass

Had gather'd.   O'er the mirror of the lake

There floated on the air pale forms of mist,

That seem'd to him, who stood beneath the verge

Of the still, incense-laden woods, the spirits
That dwell within the shadow-haunted grots
Beneath that stilly water.

      When the night
Deepen'd and darken'd o'er the changed earth,
Until the cottage on the slope above
Grew to a glimmering blot, then faded out
In gathering gloom around it; in the heart
Of Guy, who wander'd by that waveless lake,
Settled again that melancholy strange.
Why was he sad? he knew not.   That fierce war,
That raged so long, had almost pass'd away.
He doubted not that all or good or ill
Is ever ultimate good; that all may be,
By growing ever better and more wise,
Almost content and happy; that no life
Shall perish; that the veriest blade of grass
Is pregnant with the soul-life of th' All-Good,
And, though it change and wither, cannot die.
O what a sage philosopher is Love!
The soothing rhetoric of his gentle voice
Is mightier than convincing argument;

For 'tis more sweet than are, to him who plods

All day 'neath summer's sun, the deep, cool
        draughts

From shady wayside springs: his presence, smiles,

Are balmy panaceas to the heart

Sadden'd and weary, teaching it to trust

The government of all things to that Law

Supremest, that pervades the universe.

Why was he sad? he knew not.—'Tis the fate

Of those who long have suffer'd much to be

In part as they have been; the mind is slow

To break from its accustom'd trains of thought.

" Methought I heard a snatch of some sweet song,

Far-distant; sure, 'twas not the west-wind sighing—

The wind is hush'd.—Ah! yes, it is a song,

Awaking silent forest, lonely field,

Ravine, and bosky hill-side, with the heaven

Of its wild cadence. 'Tis a song I made

Long since, long since, in solitude: ah! list"—

" E'en chosen pleasures cease to please ;
  The wine of life 's a mocking cup.
Like sailors whelm'd in stormy seas,
  We grasp at straws to bear us up.
Are they not wise that are not wise,
  Who single out some thing of earth—
Some gilded plaything, paltry prize,—
  And toil, forgetting gloom and mirth,
And never see with truthful eyes
  How transient are e'en things of worth ?

" I threw a stone into the lake—
  The wavelets circled to the shore
And shook the tall, green sedgy brake,
  Then 'twas as glassy as before :
Thus roll the little waves of life,
  The deeds that mark our short career ;
The joy and woe, the peace and strife,
  Incumbent on our being here ;—
A ripple in the ocean rife—
  A moment in how many a year !"

" Would it were longer that I still might hear

That voice's music!   O how like the anthems

Of angels, heard amidst drear realms of chaos,

Was that sweet voice upon the shadowy night!

If I did know not whence it came, 'twould seem

Titania singing to King Oberon

Upon some mossy islet in the lake;

But I do know who only upon earth

Can breathe such sweetness.   O my love! my love!

'Tis thou that sing'st to let me know that thou

Art lonely waiting—waiting for my coming.

Again the heavenly magic of that voice

Falls faintly on the ear!   Yes, I will go;

It is not well that I should be alone.

She waits beneath the trees; yes, I will go—

Her love is true, true as the changeless laws

That roll the countless suns through yonder sky.

She is my world of love; with only her

In this wild, lovely wilderness of the West,

However long it is my lot to live,

Methinks I shall grow better, more content,

Till, haply in the future, mine may be
A life less sunless, days, in part, of peace."
Again, how sweetly, as he climb'd the hill,
Fell on his ear the burden of that song—

" Thus roll the little waves of life,
    The deeds that mark our short career;
The joy and woe, the peace and strife,
    Incumbent on our being here;—
A ripple in the ocean rife—
    A moment in how many a year!"

LEGEND OF THE MOXAHALA.

PREFACE.

THERE is an old story, now almost forgotten, that the Moxahala—the Indian name of a small stream that flows through the counties of Perry and Muskingum, Ohio, into the Muskingum River—derived its popular name, Jonathan Creek, from an old hunter and Indian-fighter who dwelt somewhere beside it more than a hundred years ago.   This poem is founded on that story.

Perhaps it may be asked why I have selected so obscure, local, and trivial an incident for the subject of a poem.   If this be a defect worthy of consideration, I have nothing to offer in palliation; except, if there is any merit in the verses, an observation of Wordsworth on his own poetry, "that the feeling therein developed gives importance to the action and situation, and not the action and situation to the feeling."

Though I have lately revised and materially improved this poem, as Sir Thomas More says of Richard the Third, it is still somewhat "ill-fetured of limmes." It reveals its origin; it was written at the age of nineteen. Yet, for me, it has a charm that has preserved it from the flames—the power to awaken that attribute of the mind, called by metaphysicians suggestion or association of ideas, which has such a wizard-like influence upon man, often making him happy or miserable. I never think of a line of it without remembering many a long botanical excursion, as lonely, delightful, and fruitless, judging from what I learned, as Rousseau's in his island-home, and, also, many a youthful hunting and fishing expedition, even more fruitless; for I first conceived writing it, and composed a great part of it, while angling in the stream from which it takes its name. But to others this spell will be wanting; they will view

it with the cool, discriminating eye of criticism.
Be it so. I shall be content if it has sufficient
merit to please a few and induce others, perhaps
more successful than I, to turn to a mine that is
scarcely opened,—the Indian legends of our Land
and the incidents of our early history, one of
which Campbell scorned not to sing;—tales, that
would have been the delight of Scott, if he had
been born an American, notwithstanding the curse
of our yellow-backed literature.

The brawny men of the border, both red and
white, will soon be extinct. The red man is
rapidly passing away before what, to him, is the
blight of civilization, succumbing to the law of
"the survival of the fittest;" and his antagonist,
the Indian-fighter, is to be found now only in the
wilderness of the far West. They met on the
field where General Custer with his army perished
bravely and rashly; in how many thrilling scenes
of our earlier history, recorded and unrecorded,
they have shared! With their peculiarities, vir-
tues, and vices, they are worthy the contemplation

of the philosopher; for they are phases of the eternal evolution of Nature, whose vicissitudes lead on we know not where, nor to what, in the immeasurable future.

LEGEND OF THE MOXAHALA.

I.

THE WAR-PARTY.

'Twas summer—sultry afternoon;
'Twas silent, save the wild-bee's tune;
The arrowy sunbeams, streaming down,
Gilded each tree's majestic crown,
Yet scarce within that forest-dell
A single bar of sunlight fell.
'Twas twilight there : high overhead
The aged trees their foliage spread;
And, e'en beneath them, saplings, grown
Dense through that hill-girt valley lone,
Upheld greenbriers in which there hung
The nests whére thrushes rear'd their young;
'Twas twilight there when noonday light
Blazed from the heavens' unclouded height.

137

Around a heap of embers gray—
Replenish'd not since break of day,—
In which, at morn, their meal to make
Each broil'd his savory venison-steak ;
A band of Shawnee warriors sate
In council—haughty, brave, sedate.
Far had they come from where the wave
  Of clear Scioto, gently flowing,
Reflected in its crystal pave
  The trees upon its margin growing ;
There was their village ; there old men
  Were angling in the tremulous waters :
There were their maize-fields, where, e'en then,
  Labor'd their dark-hair'd wives and daughters.

Wild turkeys' plumes, that glisten'd bright,
The raven's plumage, black as night,
And feathers, that once graced the form
Of golden eagle midst the storm,
Were woven in their ebon hair
With savage art and wondrous care.
And, painted, arm'd, and scant-array'd,
  Their sinewous limbs and osseous frames

Seem'd mightier than the men's that made
  The glory of th' Olympic games.
Long could they march, nor stop to rest;
Long could they starve, nor faint oppress'd;
The ills of savage life, the rain,
Exposure, cold, and toil (the bane
Of civilized man, who sickens, dies,
Unshelter'd from th' inclement skies),
Were their first memories; soon these grew
Almost a pleasure, for they knew
'Twas by such hardships they must grow
In strength to bend their fathers' bow,
To cast the lance, to chase the deer,
To slay the bear, nor dream of fear,
The coward vile to scorn, abhor,
To learn the sanguine art of war.

There's something in such men akin
To broad-limb'd oaks that face the din
Of many a tempest; 'neath whose shade
Their cradles, made of bark, were laid,
And where in childhood's hours they play'd.

Ay, they are brothers to the hills—
Are Nature's sons; her spirit fills
Their hearts: the ever-flowing river
Is like their footsteps, restless ever.

Cold, silent, calm, oft eloquent;
With hearts that naught can make relent,
Yet ne'er forgetful of a deed
Of kindness till is paid the meed;
Sly, cunning, cruel, yet most brave;
Too proud to plead his life to save;
E'en though his heart should break, his eye
Would shed no tear, he would not sigh;—
Such is the Indian: art and lore
   Ne'er calm'd his blood in ardor hurl'd;
Yet, once, though fallen now, he bore
   The sceptre of the Western World.

The Chieftain tall, whose plumy crest
Droop'd o'er his massy neck, address'd
His comrades thus: " Ye braves! when he,
My Father, yon bright Sun, shall be

At rest, and in the sky's soft blue
The eyes of myriad spirits view
The deeds of warriors here on earth;
Then may ye show your valor, worth.
Oft has the death-song, sad and low,
Proclaim'd the victory with the foe;
Oft have we seen our bravest fall—
What! must we perish, one and all?
The pale-face chief has slain a score,
Of late, e'en at their wigwam door;
Yes, he shall die!   The Evil Spirit
Doth fill his heart; why should we fear it?
List! souls of mighty warriors cry
For vengeance, vengeance!   He shall die.
Long did he hide we knew not where;
At last, we know the panther's lair:
Braves! on the Earth, my Mother's breast,
Let us, till dusk of evening, rest;
Then for the capture—torturing fire,
To glut our vengeance and our ire!"

Then, by the Moxahala Stream
That flow'd all-waveless like a dream
(Whose name till now was never sung
Save, haply, in the Indian tongue),
With many approving " ughs," around
They stretch'd them on the leafy ground
And summer violets.   Many slept;
  Some, smoking dreamily, watch'd the smoke
As up it circled, roll'd, and crept
  Amongst the low-bent boughs of oak;
Some fix'd their arms: but not a word
From any lip again was heard.

II.

THE INDIAN-FIGHTER AND HIS CABIN.

Hid in a dark, secluded nook
Beside where fell a moss-fringed brook
O'er pebbles white, with gurgle low,
In Moxahala Stream to flow;
A cabin, rudest dwelling, stood,
Constructed, 'neath the drooping wood,
Of logs of various size and length
Regardless save to use and strength.
And, growing o'er the bark-made roof,
Were lichens like a bison's hoof
And like the coarse and shaggy hair
That clothes the savage grizzly bear;
And with the brookside's clayey mould,
To part exclude the heat and cold,
The crannies in the log-built hut
With careless hand were roughly shut.

Upon the unhewn wall within
Hung many a silky beaver-skin;
And, on the earthen floor, the hide
Of bear and elk, full neatly dried,
Was piled—the hunter's motley bed,
With pillow soft, to rest the head,
Of panther's coat of reddish brown;
And, just above, depending down
From antlers fast against the wall,
Were pouch, that held the rifle-ball,
And powder-horn, long-used and dear,
Adorn'd with carvings quaint and queer,
And mark'd with many a mystic dot
Each for an Indian warrior shot,
Since on the Moxahala's side
Its owner, lonely, chose abide.
And in the centre ashes lay—
Collected there through many a day—
Upon a rock, whose wondrous worth
  (By playful Nature meetly shaped,)
The hunter seeing, made a hearth,
  And left a hole where smoke escaped

O'erhead the logs and bark between,
Where sweeping boughs, a leafy screen,
Dispell'd the rising smoke unseen.

In short, a mansion suited well
To him who sought that place to dwell;
Within, a low, poor, dingy room;
Without, seen through the forest-gloom
By one that off a distance stood
Amid the thick-set underwood,
It seem'd but trees, promiscuous thrown
By some dread tempest, mossy grown.

The hunter in the threshold sat
Upon a wolf-hide for a mat,
With trusty rifle close at hand
Ready to use should chance demand,—
To send his foe, if seen around,
To seek that happier hunting-ground;
And, sharing in the doorway seat
Contented at his master's feet,

Lay Don, a hound of savage breed,
Yet faithful in the hour of need;
His master's friend for many a year,
Sole sharer in his forest cheer;
The tried companion of his toil,
Partaker in the chase and spoil.

Two peers well suited to their life
Of wild adventure, border strife,
They seem'd by Nature form'd to be
Each other's only company;
For Don had grown a grade above—
Exalted by alchemic love—
The brutish fierceness of his kind;
The master had as much declined
By dwelling where no voice he heard
That spake a soft or chiding word,
Nor saw a feeling tear to flow
From eyes afire with joy or woe,
And where regard for blame and praise
Was cast away with other days:

And, thus, residing there alone
Within a world that seem'd their own,
They found an equal social sphere
That made each other doubly dear.

The woodsman was grotesquely dress'd
In Indian style; his hunting-vest,
Made by himself of half-tann'd skin,
Was gayly fringed beneath the chin
With bear-claws won in many a fray—
The blood-stain'd trophies borne away;
Around the skirt—embroidery fine—
Was many a quill of porcupine
Wrought into beads, that glisten'd bright
In various dyes 'tween black and white.
The girdle round his brawny waist,
With glittering wampum duly graced,
Held, o'er his hip, the scalping-knife
He used in close and deadly strife;
And, polish'd bright,—well did he know
To use it on his hated foe,—

His tomahawk within the band
Hung dangling ready at command.
His form, not heavy, tall and strong,
Was stoop'd by hardships suffer'd long,
Yet did his muscular limbs appear
As agile as the prairie deer;
And in his eye (that saw aright
Full many a mile past common sight,
And mark'd the least disturbance made
In mossy nook and leafy shade,
And watch'd as slow he stole around
For signs of Indians on the ground,)
There burn'd a fierce and sullen fire
   That gleams of piercing radiance shed,
Which in the bravest would inspire,
   Scarce knowing why, a thrill of dread.

His brow, where veins of blackish blue
Stood, cord-like, plainly out to view,
Was scarr'd and deeply furrow'd o'er;
And, scatter'd thin in patches hoar,
His whiskers grew without a trace
Where razor e'er had touch'd his face

And, aye, withal, he bore an air
Of settled hate or dull despair;
Yet, somehow, there was left behind
A *something*, telling to the mind
He once was loving, good, and kind!
Such in his curious scouting-gear
Was Jonathan, the pioneer;
Whose name, in those old days, to speak
Would blanch an Indian's swarthy cheek.

His surname long has been forgot.
Perchance e'en he remember'd not
That word, whate'er it was, a name
Obscure or haply known to fame,
Which in that desert ne'er again,
As whilom, fell from lips of men.
Perhaps, that name in Albion long
Was woven in many a silver song
By ladye-love for errant-knight,
    Or 'broider'd on the favor's fold
He wore in conflicts for the right
    And tournaments ablaze with gold:

And, haply, proud of lineage old
From Saxon thane or Norman bold,
His ancestors could trace their line
Through knights who fought at Palestine;
Whose graven escocheons still attest
Upon the tombs wherein they rest,
That bravely warr'd they heart and hand
'Gainst Saladin and his painim band
To rescue thence the Holy Land.
Or, yet, belike, of lineage low
Crush'd by the weight of toil and woe,
His fathers with their scanty store
Fled to a barbarous, western shore,
Pursued by priestcraft's hellish hate
With burning brand in holy state.

But why conjecture?   'Tis the same
If high or low his family-name,
So let it in oblivion sleep;
For, sure, the Shepherd knows his sheep
Though wandering in the forest deep.

III.

HIS YOUTH.

His history, gather'd here and there
From many a swain with hoary hair,
I heard in quaint and rural phrase
Told by the fireside's cheerful blaze,
And at repasts full often shared,—
By country lasses well prepared,—
Where earthen bowls, by usage brown'd,
With cider brimm'd, were pass'd around,
And home-bred worth made all elate
With joys denied the rich and great.
And, if—endeavoring here to tell
With studious care what once befell—
Imagination frame a line,
 'Twill be to blend, to give control
O'er rumors vague, and thus combine
 The lowly texture of the whole.

But be the story false or true
As told by those who never knew
The name of him they spake about
Save Jonathan, the border scout,
The moral still is worthy heed;
For every thought, and word, and deed,
Have their effects.   Who can foretell
How long they last, or ill or well?

Erst in New England dwelt a child
Upon whose birth Dame Nature smiled;
For, gifted with a love of truth
And gentle heart that others' ruth
Dissolved in sympathetic tears,
And wisdom *not* beyond his years,
He seem'd as somehow foredesign'd
   Of that most lucky, happy few,
Who, asking little, seldom find
   The pathway barren they pursue.
He was not born a Chatterton
To think, aspire, and be undone,

And, so, his boyhood was delight:
The stillness deep of summer-night,
The stirring grandeur of the storm,
The tremulous lake, the swan-like form
Of beauteous clouds, the stars, the flowers,
Possess'd for him no moving powers
Mysterious, such as some have felt;
   And, yet, no vulgar lad was he:
He loved too well; his heart would melt
   O'ermuch at others' misery.

'Tis said his home was just in sight
Of village-spires of modest white,
Whose evening bells were faintly heard;
   'Tis said his home was one of peace,
Where loving heart and loving word
   Made all but thoughts of joy to cease.
O Love, Love, Love! thou art the sole
Eden of life: thou mak'st to roll
The suns and worlds through heaven: the heart
Is happy only where thou art.

'Tis said that, 'neath green mulberry-leaves
That arch'd a lane, on summer eves,
He drove the kine (some Bess and Spot
Perchance) home from the meadow-lot,
Watching the while lest he might tread—
With shoeless foot—some pensile head
Of sweet white clover, where the bee
Droned, gathering honey ceaselessly.
And, when the luscious mulberries hung
Purple and ripe the leaves among,
He climb'd the trees and long remain'd
Till hands and lips were ruby-stain'd.
And, when the kine were milk'd and fed,
He drove them from the milking-shed
Down through the winding lane again;
Where, if the dusk was gathering then,
He hied him back from the silent spot
Afraid of—sure, he knew not what.

They say (I know not why) all day
About some mill, he used to play,

Skimming flat stones from wave to wave
Over the dam's wide-spreading pave,
With the white miller's son and daughter;
That oft he watch'd the foaming water
Dash round the creaking mossy wheel,
That whirl'd the buhr, where golden meal
And snowy wheaten flour were ground.
  Ah well, well, well! we all have seen
Life's Maydays once, and, since, have found
  Never again their like, I ween.

The boy desired to be a man.
Lo, swifter than at play he ran
In childhood's flowery, cloudless clime,
Sped on the ceaseless sands of Time;
And soon there dawn'd a wondrous change
Expanding far his mental range,
Till passion, with a deeper flow,
Made joy delight, and sorrow woe.
He felt emotions strangely strong
Conflicting ever, right and wrong,

His heart the field with battle rife;
He saw the import—risk of life.
But, still, the youth, contented not,—
All fain would choose a happier lot,—
Then sigh'd, again to be a boy,
For thoughtless hours and simpler joy.

But, gathering up his mite of care
With sweetly-smiling Hope to share
Its then but scarcely noticed weight.
While she, sweet fabler, told elate
How shortly in some happier day
The load should all be cast away,
And in its place the amaranth-flowers
Of peace, cull'd in the future's bowers,
Should make his path with beauty smile—
His heart the true Elysian Isle;
He made the best of every ill;
He conquer'd by the power of will,
And struggled on as all must do
Toward something dear to fancy's view,

And toil and pain and error met,
And oft behind him heard regret
Upbraiding for some hapless deed
When 'twas too late to e'er recede.

And when to manhood's strength he came
His life was labor still the same;
And, though full oft with sudden blight
He saw the dream Hope pictured bright
Resolved to naught, or worse, a tear;
He deem'd though 'twere through doubt, and fear,
And error, sorrow, pain, that He
    At length will lead his children home,—
From higher worlds, that they shall see
    Why darkling they were doom'd to roam.

He felt that every deed or thought
With pure intrinsic goodness fraught
Is in itself its own reward,
Though none should heed it, none accord
The plaudits due ingenuous worth;
That none can nearer reach on earth

To man's desire, felicity,
Than those whose aim it is to be,
With unremitting, noble zeal,
The furtherers true of common weal.
He saw the victor yet should wear
The guerdon olive in his hair;
And, so, he gave the hungry bread
And for the homeless found a shed;
And, lo, while soothing others' pain,
He found his loss a wondrous gain.

He loved a maid of rustic air,
But rich in beauty far more rare
Than Nature in a lavish hour
Is wont to make a mortal's dower,—
That simple treasure few possess,
A heart of genuine gentleness.

She loved him;—why was he her choice?
    I only know love's choice is right.
O oft, how oft, her low sweet voice
    Gave him, when weak, redoubled might!

For woman's weakness makes her strong;
And, with a myrtle-wand, the throng
She sways with gentle—iron will:
Ay, men, unweeting, all fulfil
Her sweet behests, though spoken low,
Resistless if her tears but flow,—
Alike inciting weal or woe.

In fancy,—as I, dreaming, raise
The spirits of old Colonial days,—
Methinks some village-bell I hear
With merry chime outpealing clear,
And see, slow moving up the aisle,
Young Jonathan with beaming smile
Conduct his blushing happy bride
Half-fearful to the altar's side,
And list the churchman's solemn rite,
Through life till death, their fates unite.

IV.

HIS HOME NEAR SENECA LAKE.

Not lavish was the husband's store,

For virtue often seeks no more

Than satisfies the present need;

And, wishing then to so proceed

That 'twould provide a cottage-farm,

And trusting to his stalwart arm

To fell the woods with patient toil

And cultivate the virgin soil;

He hied him to the lands beside

   The lone and lovely Seneca Lake,

Upon whose waveless, crystal tide,

    Then, none but Indians' oars did wake

Soft echoes, as they sought to find

    The wild duck's nest 'midst brake and reed,

Or, near the shore, to shoot the hind

    When down she came to drink and feed.

There, with the neighboring settlers' aid,
He built his cabin in the shade
Of oaks, that might have not been young
Since Cœur de Lion fought and sung.

The huge tall trees, with rumbling crash,
The pristine oak, and elm, and ash, ·
Fell prostrate 'neath his echoing stroke,
As when the Jove-hurl'd lightning broke
The giants' dread, audacious strength
And stretch'd them, quivering, at their length.
Soon fields of black-soil'd land were clear—
Whilom the covert of the deer—
Before the sturdy pioneer.

The Indian maize, with wavy leaves,
The wheat-fields, gemm'd with golden sheaves,
The fallow-land beside the rill,
The cabin on the sloping hill,
Look'd like a picture framed between
Surrounding walls of leafy green.

The mistress of that sylvan grange
Her humble household did arrange
With homely taste and ceaseless care,
Diffusing round a simple air
Of heartfelt comfort by the spell
That from her very presence fell;
For she, like Midas famed of old,
Transform'd whate'er she touch'd to gold.
And, humming some old ballad o'er
That told of far Britannia's shore,
She sped her wheel, scarce-seen, around
With sweet, continual, droning sound,
Forming with care the flaxen strand
That, woven by the self-same hand
And bleach'd beneath the solar light,
Should soon be linen snowy white:
As busy she, as poets say
Penelope, with long delay,
Chaste, laboring, wore her time away.

How wondrous are the changes wrought
Since those old days of simple thought!

Now, 'tis not meet or lady fair
    Or country lass should sit and spin;
Their work has changed.—Hark! hark! the air
    Is rent by rattling loom and gin,
Where one man does a hundred's work;
Yet all are busy: those who shirk
Are but the drones, that serve to show
What labors idlers undergo.
Ay, 'tis the age of puissant steam,
Of telegraph, and thundering beam,
And mill, and anvil, whence the hum
And stir of prospering millions come!
O Labor! thou art nobly great:
Behold each rich and populous State
Thou nurturedst up;—still westward rise
Great empires, cities, destinies!
Yes, Lincoln, splitting rails, became
The President, whose cherish'd name
Shall live—until the death of fame.

When Jonathan, with labor done
    At sultry noon or set of sun,

Turn'd homeward aye 'twas his to greet
A happy smile, a presence sweet
Awaiting at his humble door—
Ah! truly glad his toil was o'er.
And, with a kiss, as loving yet
As those in courtship none forget,
The seal of welcome was impress'd—
A balm that made his spirit rest;
O, 'tis not strange he thought him bless'd.

At night when, through the forest, shrill
Was heard the distant whip-poor-will,
Or hungry wolves' protracted howl
In answer to the hooting owl;
He told the tale of Plymouth rock
Or read his Bible—all his stock—
To her, whose knitting needles sped
The while she heard each word he said.
Thus, oft, an idle summer day,
And evening sweet with scent of hay,
And winter night when keenly blew
The north-wind down the stick-built flue,

He whiled away with legend lore
Or conn'd his Bible o'er and o'er.

With love and peace and happiness
Such as a mortal's lot might bless
(For love and virtue have the power
To fill with sunshine every hour),
They lived till years bequeath'd to them
Two blossoms like their parent stem:
A boy, in whom was plainly seen
His mother's grace, his father's mien;
And, sweeter far, with auburn curl
Shading a forehead white as pearl,
The joy of all—a lovely girl.

Ah! sweet is life whene'er it flows—
Though dash'd full oft with fleeting woes—
With love's enchantment leading where
The prospect charms, forever fair!
Is life, whose golden cynosure
Is love, that makes mankind endure
So much, so much, when deep and pure.

But, O! if Death relentless parts
With icy hands such loving hearts,
'Tis better far to be the dead
Than living when all hope is fled—
Than feel 'twere bliss to ne'er have known
The heaven of love, forever flown,
When left with woe, alone! *alone!*—

'Twas autumn, when the mellow air
A sense of sadness seem'd to bear,
And leaves of gorgeous red and brown
And burnish'd gold fell rustling down,
And o'er the distant hills a band
Of gossamer haze seem'd fairyland;
That beauteous season few e'er know
Save in Columbia's autumn glow,
When deep Enchantment weaves around
Her spells in every sight and sound
Till Nature's self is full of rhyme,—
The Indian's soft-air'd Summer-time.

The eve had pass'd, and midnight shade
Profound hung over wood and glade,

And stars aloft were twinkling bright,
And softly sigh'd the wind of night;
Nor at the cabin, looming dim
'Neath many a drooping, shadowy limb,
Was felt the least portent of ill
Where, save the night-bird, all was still.

But, suddenly, howl and horrid yell
As from the confines dim of hell,
And helpless shriek, and dying wail,
Fell mingling on the shuddering gale!
And, in the cabin, all afire,
Uprose the red man's whoop of ire—
While tomahawk and scalping-knife
Dealt common death to child and wife!
And, dancing wild, with menace dread
And eagle-plumes upon each head
And war-paint daub'd in hideous streak
With mystic power o'er brow and cheek,
The warriors, 'midst the spectral glare,
Fierce, terrible demons of despair,
Brandish'd their scalps of gory hair!

Long had the din of havoc ceased;
And, rising in the orient east,
The sun look'd down as bright, serene,
O'er smouldering logs and ruin'd scene,
And woodland life, unheeding, gay,
Pursued its self-same destined way,
As if no heart was crush'd with grief
To which but death could give relief.

Yes, Jonathan—unconscious how—
Escaped, though gash'd across the brow;
For 'twas his fate to struggle on
Though hope had flown—forever gone:
And there he stood and could not weep,
Wan, woful, haggard! by the heap,—
The ruins of his home,—the grave
  Of children, wife, to ashes burn'd;
There all he loved and could not save
  Lay in the dying embers urn'd!
And, bowing low with no desire
Save death beside that funeral pyre,

His quivering voice, so long suppress'd
By choking anguish in his breast,
Burst forth in wail and hopeless moan.
"Oh God! why am I left alone?
When all are dead I cherish dear
'Tis death—'tis death to linger here!
O! would that fate had will'd that I,
With those I love, should live--and die!"

He heeded not the comfort given
By many a heart with pity riven;
And soon his wavy hair was gray.
Then from his eye a vengeful ray
Gleam'd out, of unrelenting hate;
And then he half-forgot his fate,
Oft, like a madman, cruel smiled;
And people deem'd his fancy wild.—
Ere chill November came and went,
From out that border settlement
With ammunition, hound, and gun
(Telling his future course to none),
He turn'd him toward the Setting Sun.

V.

THE LAST CONFLICT.

The sun had set; the crescent moon
With halo wan had follow'd soon;
And Moxahala, shadow'd o'er
By buckeye, beech, and sycamore,
Flow'd gurgling 'neath the gloom of night;
And, 'tween the leaves that rippled light,
Look'd, trembling, here and there a gleam
Of starlight on the dimpling stream.

With piercing glance and noiseless tread
Quick from his hut the hunter fled
(While Don, as stealthful, keeping nigh
Glared fiercely round with savage eye),
For, having cross'd the woody vale,
He came upon an Indian trail

And all his deadly peril felt:
Well did he know the place he dwelt
Was sought by Indians far and near—
To wreak revenge—for many a year.

The Shawnee Chief had track'd the bear,
At last, e'en to his hidden lair.
And, stealing from the bosky glen
With half a hundred ruthless men,
Before 'twas his the foe to take
He mentally burn'd him at the stake
For many a murder'd warrior's sake.

The red men, feeling sure the prey
Was in his fastness brought to bay,
Closed round the hut on every side;
And some the fiery brand applied,
While others, yelling, turn'd to bind
The dreadful foe they thought to find,
And rush'd within with tiger-bound—
But, lo! no captive there they found.

Hark! ringing on the midnight breeze
Afar 'neath labyrinthian trees,
A rifle shrieks with sulphurous breath
Sending its message dire of death—
The Shawnee Chief with dying whoop
Falls, quivering, midst the motley group.
Ha! now amazement dumb appalls—
A sharp report—another falls—
O pale-face Chief, away! away!
Loud, fierce, resounds the deep-voiced bay
Of ghoulish forms, a horrid pack,
That, howling, bound upon your track
With bow and spear and gun and knife
And tomahawk to take your life!
Away—away—go, seek the cave
Where oft before, your life to save,
With mystery deep, you did elude
The hordes that at your back pursued.
Ah hark! they come with sounding tread
And whoops that echo wild and dread!—

*   *   *   *   *   *   *   *

Dewy, and fragrant-breath'd, and pale,
  Came morn, with wakening voice of bird
And bee, and cool leaf-stirring gale,
  And squirrel's chirp, mid branches, heard.

'Twas on a hill-side's bluffy edge,
Where rocks stuck out with mossy ledge,
Where wavy-scallop'd ferns between
The fissured rocks grew rich and green,
And delicate flowers, to us unknown
Save—hid from man—in forests lone,
Bloom'd 'neath the trees that, arching high,
Shut out the azure summer sky.

Where ivy wild and grapevines clung
To drooping shrubs that overhung
The lichen'd rocks and shady ground,
Beneath the ledge a passage wound,
That, to a cavern dark and small,
Led through a jagged, narrow hall.
There Jonathan the night before
  Escaped the Indians in his flight;

He seem'd to vanish—be no more!
  And they, with awe and sore affright
And superstitious fancy fraught,
Deem'd 'twas a demon they had fought,
And hied them homeward full of thought.

But Jonathan lay cold and dead,
The cavern-floor his rocky bed;
And on his bosom, clotted o'er
With oozy drops of blackish gore,
A ball had left its circle red;
And in his back an arrow-head,
With shaft protruding, broke in two,
Had proved its fatal guidance true.
Yes, Jonathan, the pale-face Chief,
Had found at last that sweet relief—
Nepenthe for each earthly grief.
And e'en o'er him *one* mourner kept
His vigil—yea, and, haply, wept;
For think not man alone can know
The bliss of love, the pang of woe:—

With paws upon his master's breast
And plaintive howl of deep unrest,
His lonely dog, though all unheard,
Implored a look, a loving word,
And lick'd his master's cheek and hand,
And seem'd to vaguely understand
His soul was in a happier land!

OLELA:

A WANDERER'S VISION OF PEACE.

OLELA:

A WANDERER'S VISION OF PEACE.

I.

Continuous, falling, falling, falling,
I heard the rain
Against the pane
So drearily to wax and wane;
And loneliness, both vague, appalling,
Seem'd everywhere
To clog the air
Like some foreboding of despair;
Yet, while—that stormy night—my heart was teeming
With fancies fell,
I knew full well,
E'en while I could not break the spell

(For Psyche told me truly), 'twas but seeming :
Upon her breast
She bade me rest,
And there I laid me dreaming.

II.

I dwelt within a valley's space—
The homestead of a rural race;
A cot my happy dwelling-place,
With mossy thatch and arbor-tree;
And round the vale on either side
A wall of mountains, azure-dyed,
Was rear'd aloft to ever hide
And guard its pure simplicity.

III.

And through the valley, clover red
And forest-phlox with nodding head
A soft, delicious fragrance shed,
As in some blossomy nook of Aidenn;

And o'er the flowers a busy brood
Of wild-bees cull'd ambrosial food,
Or droned a drowsy interlude
   When homeward bound with honey laden.

IV.

There, arch'd by willows all the way,
Where cattle dozed the summer-day
And wind-flowers blossom'd all the May,
   A mountain brook with pebbly strand
(The child of many a bright cascade),
Beneath the tremulous light and shade,
Went dancing to the pipe it play'd
   Adown the sheep-cropp'd meadow-land.

V.

And, hid deep in the copsy dell,
On upland slope, and grassy fell,
Was heard the sweetly tinkling bell
   With echo faint, from flocks of sheep;

And near—while o'er the thymy ground
With busy lip and munching sound
The sheep would nip the herbage round—
  The shepherd loiter'd, half asleep.

VI.

There vain Ambition never came,
The high and low were all the same—
Life's frugal wants the proudest aim,—
  And care return'd not with the dawn ;
For Luxury was all unknown,
And Pride had long been overthrown
By Love, that reign'd supreme, alone ;
  Thus life's still current dimpled on.

VII.

In spring-time when the fields were green,
The valley held a festive scene
Where lad and lass with smile serene
  Wove garlands in each other's hair ;

And, roving far in search of flowers—
The blushing maids like rosy Hours,—
Were thrill'd by love's bewitching powers,
  And then were doubly, doubly fair.

VIII.

And in the drowsy summer weather
They pitch'd the odorous hay together,
And gather'd lilies in the heather
  While resting through the sultry noon;
And when at last the sun-tann'd hay
For all the year was mow'd away,
The youths and maids, with laughter gay,
  Would dance beneath the misty moon.

IX.

When Autumn, far more lavish, bold,
Than alchemists renown'd of old,
Transform'd the very woods to gold;
  They roam'd the hills with forest grown

And gather'd—as they patter'd down
From many a treetop's gorgeous crown—
The ripen'd nuts, as russet brown
    As were the lasses' tresses blown.

X.

And when, at night, the angry blast
With ghostly footfalls, moaning, pass'd
Round sylvan grange, and wildly cast
    Fantastically the sifting snow;
By cheerful firesides through the vale
True lovers told that sweetest tale,
And quite forgot the wintry wail
    In bliss that only lovers know.

XI.

What lofty calling is so great
As that of him, of low estate,
Who, asking ne'er a change of fate,
    Dwells far away from heartless pride,

And, mingling not in fashion's coil,
Sees pleasure pure in healthful toil,—
To prune the tree and till the soil
   And fold the herd at even-tide?

XII.

For sure content is almost heaven;
And he, to whom such wealth is given,
Is bless'd beyond who long has striven
   While love of grandeur fired his breast.
Ah, yes! give me the rustic cot,
The meadow, wold, and garden plot,—
The glory of a lowly lot,
   Where Peace may come and build her nest!

XIII.

In that sweet dale with one, a friend,
I many a happy hour would spend
Till eve, when glimmering shadows blend
   Shutting the landscape from the eye;

As angling in some willowy nook—
Like Walton erst at Shawford-brook,—
With converse low and busy hook
　　We knew not hours were fleeing by.

XIV.

My home—most dear beyond degree!
In highest heaven, it seems to me,
If souls are bless'd as souls *can* be,
　　Each has a dear, delightful home,
'Neath towering trees that sigh above,
'Midst birds and flowers and hearts to love,—
The dovecot to the carrier-dove
　　When, weary, it has ceased to roam!

XV.

There Olela, the light of all,
Who held my chosen heart in thrall,
Dispell'd, e'en by the fairy fall
　　Of her soft footsteps, every care;

And, as the clouds beneath the sun

Grow luminous that were dark and dun,

She smiled—and homeliest objects won

   A kindred radiance, rich and rare!

XVI.

In laugh and motion, form and face,

She bore that untaught native grace

That Goethes dream and Raphaels trace—

   Ah, rarely found upon the earth;

And loveliest, most majestic part

Of perfect beauty, void of art,—

The heaven within a guileless heart

   That overflows with love and worth!

XVII.

Full oft beneath the dark green leaves

Of vines that wreathed our cottage-eaves,

At evening, when the earth receives

   A pensive stillness, mystic spell,—

We spake a language silent, sweet;
And while our hearts with passion beat
Our eyes were with a tale replete
   That voice could never speak so well.

XVIII.

Her speech was music soft and low,
The tongue that love should ever know;
And, if she sung, a tear would flow--
   Celestial portals stood ajar.
Ah! 'mid the myriad flowers of spring
Fann'd by the zephyr's scented wing,
Again, methinks, I hear her sing
   These stanzas to the Evening Star:

XIX.

I.

Pale Star! that shimmer'st o'er yon mountain peak
   While yet the sky
Is tinged, like some shy maiden's blushing cheek,
   With crimson dye,

2.

So long before another star is seen
> To tremble through,
With faint, faint spark, the heaven's serene
> Unclouded blue,—

3.

How beautiful thou art!   What hallow'd calm
> Of memories dear
Thou bring'st and pour'st upon us—sweet, if balm,
> Or, cause of tear!

4.

'Tis deem'd thine is the hour when lovers learn
> To dream and sigh,
And hearts, while stolen, all-meaning kisses burn,
> Throb warm and high.

5.

Coy vestal Eve, enrobed in gray and brown,
> Thyself dost love;
Else, why, when *she* is here, dost *thou* smile down
> From heaven above?

6.

Thy golden beam is not all joy alone;
　　E'en though thou shine,
For aye, upon thy love from yon high throne,
　　She'll ne'er be thine!

7.

Ah, yes! e'en now, thy pensive influence fills
　　The twilight air,
That, kissing all the roses' cheeks, distils
　　In tear-drops there.—

8.

By thy soft light, that brightens more and more
　　As shadows fall,
Here, let me bow beneath the sky—adore
　　The Soul of All!

XX.

Yes, home is more than all beside,
'Tis where the saintliest hopes abide:
My cot, where time would swiftly glide
　　Yet be an endless merry May,

Was all a world of love to me,

A fairy isle far 'midst the sea

Where care and woe could never be,—

   Enchantment smiled them all away.

XXI.

For, waiting ever, Love would stand

For Olela's most sweet command;

And wheresoe'er she placed her hand

   She left the charm of beauty's power,

Ennobling toil and rural life

Beyond the madding din and strife

And envy, like a demon, rife

   Within the prince's pennon'd tower.

XXII.

O! who, on earth, can be more bless'd

Than he that, in a loving breast

(A universe—and all possess'd),

   Is cherish'd 'mid some scene of peace?

Such simple life, all bliss ·the same,

Such true content, without a blame,

Are more than all the vaunted fame

   And glory of both Rome and Greece!

XXIII.

I waked——   And, driving, driving, driving

   Before the gale,

   The heavy hail

Struck pane and roof, amidst the wail

Of trees and winds in conflict striving;—

   And, ah! my heart

   Without a start

Felt storm and night its counterpart,

Nor, from my worn and weary Soul, could borrow

   A golden gleam,

   A hopeful beam

To stream within so dark a dream—

No radiant vision of a bright to-morrow!

   For life, to me,

   Where'er I be,

The *past* hath fill'd with sorrow.

MISCELLANEOUS POEMS.

OURANOPETES.

I.

I REMEMBER—and thus I am cursed.
O how sweet were a Lethean measure
To deaden the memory of Pleasure
When the bright-tinted bubble is burst!
When dreams, that, while *dreaming*,
Seem teeming
With bliss,
Are no more;
Ah! why are we doom'd to deplore
That *something* we ever shall miss?

II.

To live is to dream hath been said:
Oh! the phantoms that flit without number

Through the dusk of that feverish slumber—
Perchance 'tis to *wake* to be *dead?*
Some dreams there are stranger,
And change ere
The rest;
It is well
Not all are predestined to dwell
In that land—or blasted or bless'd.

III.

Dare I tell of a Being most fair,
On whose face of all beauty for hours
I gazed, 'neath the tremulous showers
Of her tropical sunshine of hair?—
Till her presence it fill'd me,
Near kill'd me
With love;
Nor I knew
That a Being so bright was untrue,—
They had cast her from heaven above.

IV.

O her eyes were so lustrous and wild!
  Their cerulean strangeness—their glances
  Enchain'd me in magical trances;
Ah, I knew not their light was defiled.
    And her hands were so slender

                    And tender

                    And white;

      What a thrill,

      When I press'd them, they gave,—'twas

      a chill

Of intoxicating, 'wildering delight!

V.

We were wandering one morn in a wood:
  From the fruit-laden branches all mossy,
  Hung parasites, crimson and glossy,
Shedding fragrance around where we stood;
    In that forest enchanted,

                    O'erflaunted

                    The sod,

Weeping dew,
   Every blossom delicious that grew
In the river-fed Garden of God.

VI.

We were loitering alone in a wood:
   I had drunk of her Circean sweetness—
   The nectar of gods in completeness;
She had kiss'd me e'en there as we stood.—
   Where was she?   Lo, dimmer

            Did glimmer

            The dawn

   From the skies,
      For my day was the light of her eyes:—
She had vanish'd—oh! where had she gone?

VII.

How sweetly, from far through the trees,
   Echo'd peals of her musical laughter!
   "I will fly," then I cried, "follow after"—
But white lilies entangled my knees.

Her mantle of whiteness,

Her brightness
Of hair

I could see,

Fluttering wildly past many a tree,

As she sail'd like a god on the air.

VIII.

In that forest were streamlets of light

Dancing on under thickets of roses ;

There were dim-lighted labyrinths and closes,

Though the sun arose glorious and bright :

And around me was ringing

The singing
Of birds,

Whose wild glee

Cast a mystical sadness o'er me,—

They were carolling sibylline words.

IX.

All day, through that wilderness strange,

I follow'd the Soul of my vision—

Was led by a Laugh of derision
In a world of enchantment and change.
When twilight descended,

　　　　　　　Attended

　　　　　　　Despair

On my heart;
And I knew it would never depart,
For a demon did prophesy there.

X.

Then the stars became lurid and fierce,—
　　Like tiger-eyes, hunger'd their fires;
　　And the myrtle grew thistles and briers;
And each blossom all thorny to pierce:
　　Yet I follow'd, unheeding

　　　　　　　And bleeding,

　　　　　　　That Voice

In the night,
Though it rung with a fiendish delight,—
Alas! it bereft me of choice.

XI.

At length, e'en the stars overhead,

　　Despising my terrible anguish,

　　Began to appallingly languish—

And soon they were rayless and dead!

　　　Then hopelessness rushing

　　　　　　　　Came crushing

　　　　　　　　Me low;

　　　And I pray'd

　　　The Destroyer would hear me and aid,

And swoon'd in the midnight of woe.

XII.

It seem'd as if æons had flown

　　Exceeding in vastness the ages

　　Of the world with its rock-written pages,—

Perchance, 'twas a moment alone,—

　　　When a Power bent o'er me

　　　　　　　　And bore me

　　　　　　　　To earth:

I awoke,

But my spirit was humbled and broke;

And life was not life but a dearth.

XIII.

Now my soul it doth hunger and thirst

For a Being of exquisite beauty,

Whom to worship did seem but a duty,

But whose smile is a sorcery accursed.—

When dreams, that, in seeming,

Are teeming

With bliss,

Become woe;

O God! 'twere a heaven below

To forget what we ever shall miss.

LINCOLN:

AN ODE.

'Εντάφιον δὲ τοιοῦτον οὔτ' εὐρὼς

οὔθ' ὁ πανδαμάτωρ ἀμαυρώσει χρόνος. . . . .

SIMONIDES.

I.

THERE is no earthly word or deed

More worthy heaven, Prometheus-like, sublime,

Than his who, deeming death the meed,

Undaunted, calm, speaks trúth condemning crime,

And, 'mid unnumber'd foes,

Injustice dares oppose.

II.

O! 'tis most sweet, when life seems vain,

And doubts appall, and tears are fain to flow,

To feel that Man may here attain
Such heights exalted in this world of woe!
    Acts angels stoop to view—
    Yea, might aspire to do.

III.

LINCOLN! thy name shall ever shine
A beacon bright amid our nether gloom.
    Till Freedom, Virtue perish, *thine*
Shall be a theme of praise—an envied doom;
    And Greatness bend the knee,
    Though emulous, to thee.

IV.

How few, how few have graced the earth
Whose names with thine 'tis justice to unite.
    Where is thy peer for simple worth?
Who like to thee 'mid danger's darkest night?
    Serene whate'er thy fate;
    Without ambition, great.

v.

Thou second Founder of thy land!

Small need hast thou of choral hymns of praise;

Thy vindicating heart and hand

Wove thee bright wreaths of never-dying bays,

That blossom full as fair

Though twined not in thy hair.

vi.

Thou smot'st the shackles from the slave,

Didst slay a demon, bid a curse depart;

Thou fill'st, alas! a martyr's grave,

Though sepulcher'd within thy Nation's heart!

Thy monument thy name,

Festoon'd with deathless fame.

vii.

'Tis well to weep when those are dead

Who make the world not better ere they go;

But, when great saintly souls have fled

High heavenward, let no heart a sorrow know,—

But swell with joy and pride

That such have lived and died!

SOLILOQUY

I'VE traversed scenes renown'd in song,
   I've mix'd with pomp and chivalry,
   Yet dearest is this·spot to me,
This simple spot, remember'd long.

Canst thou be dead, my playmate? thou
   Whose name is link'd with youth's delight?
Ah, Maud! methinks I see thee now
   With eyes and tresses dark as night.

Below those hills where jut the rocks
   Above yon shady mountain stream,
   And, dim as objects in a dream,
Are mirror'd back in massy blocks,—

We gather'd lilies on the ledges,
   That, as Narcissus loved of eld,
Bow'd coyly o'er the mossy edges
   To view themselves as he beheld.

'Tis strange, though thou art pass'd away,
   That Nature smiles the same as then ;—
   E'en heaven's white cloudlets sail again
Just as we watch'd them when at play.

Ah, Childhood—flowery May of life
   That swiftly passes toward December,
And only leaves 'mid after strife
   Thy sinless raptures to remember—

How truly sweet thy transient day !
   Who can but scarce repress a tear
   While thinking when nor care nor fear
Cast shadows o'er life's sunny way ?

Oh for a spell to vanquish fate—
　Her woven woof of woes to sever,—
I'd live a life with joy elate
　A thoughtless child, how happy ever.

For, but in merry childhood, dance
　The sunbeams, leaves, and gurgling streams
　(More rapturous than heaven-pictured dreams),
With *all* their beauty and romance.

Yes, we may live and toil and learn
　And fancy we are growing wise,
But, still, methinks we ever yearn
　To see again with childish eyes!

Ah, Maud, with patience unexcell'd
　We angled here for mountain trout,
　And hail'd their capture with a shout
Whose echo up the valley swell'd;

While I, with self-important look,
    Would act the true gallant the while,
And fix for thee the bearded hook
    Repaid by an approving smile.

And oft together by the hour
    We read some witching fairy-tale,
    How fairy-knights, encased in mail,
Would scale their ladies' dizzy tower;

Then, gathering loosen'd stones and moss,
    We'd build a castle grand and gray,
And moat it with a frowning fosse
    To guard its portals night and day;

And thou wouldst be the princess fair,
    Confined by some magician's doom
    To wait within the castle's gloom
The knight who would its dangers dare.

Then, storming battlement and wall
　　Right nobly, with a knightly mien,
I razed the fortress, court and hall,
　　To rescue thence the captive Queen.

Was it not joy—earth's purest bliss?
　　Though childish pleasures long are pass'd
　　I'll still remember to the last
The sweetness of a boyish kiss!

Well—well—perchance, from some sweet star,
　　Which haply is a heaven for thee,
Thou seest me now, sad, lone, afar,
　　And shed'st, e'en there, a tear for me.

AN HOUR OF SLUMBER.

DEEP silence reigns;—it is the hour of slumber;

And o'er how many a heart the drowsy wizard

Is weaving now his wondrous woof of phantasy.

Some are most happy;—hopes they long have

    cherish'd

Are bursting into flower, yea, soon to ripen

And be but nothing. One doth kiss his sweetheart;

Another has his riches—vain Golconda!

Another reck'd of fame,—the Iris-bubble

Is thricely sweeter than if it were real.

Some wander in a mystic land of Faerie

Where everything becomes just what it is not;

And others—so this wizard has decreed it—

Oh, what they suffer! death and hell and torture.

This one has slain his father, and for nothing;

That one is to be hang'd by those that love him;

Another plunges down a frightful chasm.

But ah! most sad of all, some hear their conscience

Upbraiding for the crimes they have committed.

HYMN TO THE OCEAN.

Unconquerable Titan! chainless Sea!
Thou wild expanse of waters, bluer far
Than heaven that stoops to meet thy seeming
     verge,—
Embodiment of grandeur,—beauteous world
Of warring waves, too great for thought to grasp
Thy dread infinitude,—O Sea! at length,
Once more, I cast me at thy feet, and feel
My heart to throb in concord with thy dark
Deep-sounding billows.   Thou dost dash thy surf,
Wave after wave, upon the craggy beach,
Whose foam seethes hissing over shell and sand,
As if to greet me :—thy hoarse-murmuring voice
Hath bid me welcome!   O, how oft, amid
The inland hills and valleys of the West,
Have I, like some fond lover, dream'd of thee,—
In fancy, stretch'd me e'en as now I lie

Upon thy chafed and weed-strown sands to gaze

Upon thy darkling waters, and have drifted

At thy wild will, I knew not, cared not where,

Happy while seeming pillow'd on thy breast.—

Immutable Ocean! of all things of earth,

Thou art most constant.   Man doth feel the thrills

Of love, delight, and hope; but they depart

Or perish: he is worn and crush'd beneath

Sorrow and care and toil and misery;

But they are loth to leave him, and he dies.

Nations arise to fall; the wilderness

Blossoms a garden, and doth change again

To wood or desert; e'en the very Earth

Varies her aspect; mountain-tops fall prone

Before the earthquake, valleys rise aloft

Again to sink, and rivers fade away——

Thou, thou, alone, dost change not. Though thou smil'st

And frown'st and smil'st again, 'tis wantonness

In mockery of th' inexorable doom

Of all save thee.

Relentless, fell Destroyer,
Yet Guardian of how many a myriad lives—
A universe thou art within thyself!
Thine offspring are innumerable; the stars,
That on thy hyaline vastness nightly gaze,
Are not their equal.—E'en thy very sands
Are fill'd with countless beings, and thy depth
Is the unbounded habitation, realm,
Of monster-forms, from the leviathan,
More huge than aught that treads upon the earth,
To the insensate polyp.   This fair shell,
That dwelt amid thine uproar, rudely thrown
From thy deep-throbbing bosom to my feet,
Is the diminutive mansion of a life.
And thou hast, 'neath thy waters, oozy leas,
Paved with bright silver sands and milky pearls
And rainbow-tinted shells and gems that gleam
With tremulous radiance in thy shadowy depths,—
Caves dark as Erebus, the dread abode
Of solitude and thine eternal waves,—
Huge towering Alps, whose wildly-clifted sides,
Hoary with shaggy moss, hang terrible

Amid thy waters,—quiet dells o'ergrown
With waving sea-blooms, fairy spots of strange
Fantastic loveliness,—and coral-groves,
Branching with shapeless foliage, old as thou :
And o'er thy waters many a wilderness
Of tangled seaweed drifts in calm and storm.

Thine azure waves roll on continuously ;
They dance at pleasure round how many a shore—
True nymphs of freedom, curbless as the wind.
Their children are the clouds that people heaven ;
They wanton with them, mocking all their smiles
And frowns alternate in thy glassy depth :
The rainbow is their daughter, beauteous spirit
Smiling 'mid storms, begotten of the sun.
Thy billows, through the watches of the night,
Mirror the sky's cerulean pave, and read
Its starry pages sinking to the west,—
The Magi of the ocean.   When the moon,
Beautiful sorceress, doth smile beyond
Thine either verge, thy waters heave and swell
In tremulous splendor, save when some far wave

With opaline undulation, for an instant,
Seems to o'erwhelm her,—follow'd, startlingly,
By an intenser spell of her enchantment.

Most puissant Element! whose lacy foam
Cradled the Goddess of all-conquering Love,
It is not strange thine is the wondrous realm
Imagination fill'd with sinewous gods,
And fair Dorissan beings, whose nude forms,
Ineffable in loveliness, did rival
Their heavenly sisters.   Musing on thy bright
Alhambran grottoes, gleaming shell-strown ways,
And Vallombrosan dales festoon'd with moss,
Thou seem'st the dwelling-place of deities,—
A world where blessed souls might choose abide,
Leaving Elysium.   Ah! methinks I see
Sweet slumbering Nereids, couch'd in glimmering
        caves,
Their scallop-shells unstrung and by them laid;
While, o'er their bosoms, azure-tinted locks,
Begemm'd with sapphire, pearl, and amethyst,
Ripple upon the water.—Fancy, now,

Pictures thy monarch hoar, careering on

Over thy prairies vast, his chariot-wheels

Hurling a sheen of sprayey gems! while, hark,

Old Triton winds his charmed horn to soothe

Thy troublous deep.

                Thyself, resistless Power!

In thy sublime vicissitudes, in thine

Omnipotence, and ever-during youth,

And might, and beauty, seem'st a god.   Thou

     reck'st

Not for the mightiest of this wide, wide world.

With thy tempestuous voice thou laugh'st to scorn

The puny mandates even of a Xerxes;

His pennon'd navies, boasting of their might,

Planning the blood-bought conquest of an empire,

Thou playfully dost shatter—dash to naught,

Nor deign'st thou give account to earthly power.

Thy days are as thy bleach'd unnumbered sands,

And yet thou art not older,—still the same

In glory and in grandeur; time, to thee,

Is but the chronicler of thine eternity.

Æons on æons, in the unmeasured past,

When there was not a man to write, thou kept'st

The annals of the childhood of the world.

Nature's most lowly children thou didst mark

To grow and multiply, through centuries,

And change, till many vanish'd from the earth;

Yet in thy rocky tablets thou inscrib'dst

Their various history.   Strange, unwieldy shapes,

That now have not their counterpart on earth,

Paddled upon thy waters, and became,

In ages, parents of new progeny;

Yet thou preserv'dst their memory, and didst trace

Their curious lineage, O thou hoariest Sage!

Save Time.   Nor wert thou idle then; thou rear'dst,

Through those dim awful vacuums, rocks on rocks,

Foundations of new worlds where yet should teem

Strange beings, flowers, and verdure.   Thou didst
        take

The earth, e'en as a giant, in thine arms—

Moulding her form and destiny.   O when

The mind doth seek to grasp such mighty
        thoughts—

Such magnitude, 'tis palsied, falling spent,

E'en as the little land-bird falls and dies

'Midst thy unbounded vastness.   Aged Sea!

A being of an hour, I muse upon

Thy past and future, lost in thee and Nature——

When thou dost writhe convulsed, almighty Being!

In agony of passion, and the heavens

Darken above thee;—when thy boundless plains

Are plow'd by tempests, rolling up thy waves

To mountain-billows, and the sea-flowers quake

With terror and are shatter'd in thy depths;—

When the quick lightning, demon of the storm,

Leaps zigzag, making palpable the gloom

And desolation, follow'd by the roll

Of thunders deepening, 'midst contending voices

Of winds and waves!—when the tried mariner

Grows pale with fear and trembles at the helm;—

O, then, how terribly beautiful, sublime

Thou art, O Uncontrollable!—Yet lull'd,

As now thou slumber'st conscious of thy strength,

Thou art how lovely, grand, bright summer Sea!

While gently heave thy billows, bounding on
With ever-changing, calm magnificence,
Beneath the dancing sunlight.

                      I would dwell,
O murmuring Ocean! ever dwell with thee,
And be thy low companion.   I would rove
Thy stern precipitous cliffs, and yesty beach,
And by thy rocky coves, and lonely bays,
To gather shells which thou wouldst bring to me.
I would forget the world, forget myself,
And care and pride, and, here alone with thee,
Be *almost* happy.—I do love to study
Thy changing moods; when placid, dream with
      thee,—
When madding, feel my heart swell like thy waves
Tempestuously.   Ah, yes, 'tis sweet to mark
The osprey circle heavenward and swoop down
To snatch his finny prey,—to feel thy breath
Fanning my cheek,—to watch, at morn and even,
The level sunshine cast its magic woof
Of mingled Tyrian, golden, roseate dyes
O'er thy upheaving surface.   'Tis delight

To gaze full oft upon thy breaker-bars'
White caps of feathery foam,—to hear thy roar
And mingle with thy tumult! for thy voice,
Replete with harmony, invokes to life
Th' enthusiasm of childhood, and thou speak'st
A wordless language touching mystic things.

I would cast off this being to become
An atom of thy grand immensity,—
To catch the ardor of thy freedom,—feel
Thy soul to stir within me!   O to be
The spume upon thy ever-rolling surf,—
A weed to toss upon thee aimlessly,—
A wave to feel thy impetus and throb
With thy pulsations, rocking far from shore,
The lonely petrel nursling of the deep.—
Oh that I were the viewless, fitful gale,
Rising in tempests—spirit, wild and free,
Thy seemly playmate, ever dancing on
Over thy shimmering wilderness of waves!
Take me upon thy breast, impetuous Sea—
·Bear me afar to some balm-breathing isle

Lapp'd in thy murmur, O symphonious One,
Only with thee to dwell, for aye, and muse
Upon thy music, beauty, glory, grandeur—
Only with thee, dark OCEAN! sounding SEA.

SUMMER DAYS.

How sweet it is, when summer days
   Pass stilly like delicious dreams,
To traverse unfrequented ways
   Where murmur cooling sylvan streams,
And faintly catch the mellow sound
   Of voices far, in dreamy mood,
And fancy in some shade profound
   The genii of the solitude
Are holding, as the Indians tell,
Their war-dance in some haunted dell:

And, when sweet fragrance fills the air
   From many a milky elder-bloom,
To lie far from the sunny glare
   Beneath some beech-wood's pleasant gloom,

Or, loitering on for hours and hours
    Where o'er the treetops squirrels run,
To gather scattering forest flowers
    In valleys pied with shade and sun,
While echoing softly round is heard
    The song of thrush and mocking-bird.

HYMN

TO THE INCOMPREHENSIBLE.

WHEN Sorrow drapes me in her pall,
And dread Despair broods over all ;
When Pleasure thrills with warm delight,
And Beauty charms, Astarte-bright ;
Yea, in all time—in Winter bare,
When Summer's tresses scent the air ;—
O Thou ! whate'er thy name may be,
Father of all, I bow to Thee !

However sad my low estate,
I ask not oft a happier fate.
One life—what is it when 'tis o'er ?
An atom Time has dash'd ashore !

20

Its toil may be another's rest;
Its woe be haply for the best.
Weak, weary, though I cannot see—
Ruler of all, I bow to Thee!

O Thou! who, soul-like, dost pervade
The universe, unbounded made,
In whose mysterious laws we see
The majesty of divinity,—
O Thou! unseen, not understood,
Inscrutable—yet all wise and good,—
In every fate, whate'er it be,
Soul of all Life! I bow to Thee!

THE AZTEC MAIDEN.

A SCENE BY THE LAKE NEAR THE ANCIENT
CITY OF TENOCHTITLAN.

Watching many an island, slowly
    Floating 'neath th' o'ershadowing mountains
O'er the lake, where, drooping lowly,
    Tropic ferns kiss'd murmuring fountains,
'Neath the trees, a shadowy bower,
    Sat a lovely Aztec Maiden,
While the air, from many a flower,
    With delicious fragrance laden,
Waved her long and raven tresses
Like a lover's fond caresses.
Sitting where the mossy ledges
Ever dripp'd, she watch'd the sedges

Rise and fall above the swallow,
Bathing in its pearly hollow,
While her fingers idly braided
Garlands sweet of flowers unfaded.

Ah! she seem'd a Dryad dreaming,
    While the west-wind, fain to fold her,
Kiss'd her through her tresses streaming
    Over bosom, brow, and shoulder;
And how lovely! for the fever
    In her young blood, warmly gushing,
Dancing on, did always leave her
    Fair as northern maidens *blushing*,—
Yea, like fruits where skies are sunny,
    Ripen'd deep, whose juices bloody
Through the rind (like Hybla's honey)
    Look so tempting, rich and ruddy!
Loop'd with buds, her mantle flowing
Hid her knees; all round and glowing
Lay her limbs almost revealing
Charms, that moss and flowers, concealing,

Seem'd as conscious 'twas a blessing
To droop over—touch—caressing.

Thus she sat a wreath entwining
On her arm at ease reclining,
When, perchance, remember'd pleasure
(Sweet is memory's hoarded treasure)
Made her olive features fairer—
Blushing made their beauty rarer,—
Like a summer sea by moonlight,
Like a mountain's snow at noonlight,
Or the rainbow's tinted shading,
Brightly coming, softly fading ;—
For she thought of Maspaola,
Of the chieftain Maspaola.
Though the airs of female-college
Ne'er had added to her knowledge,
Love, that oldest, sweetest story,
Had its chosen knight of glory,—
And by whose emotion, moving
All her heart, how truly proving

That, though southern suns had kiss'd her,
All must own her as a sister.

Scattering flowers, she rises stately
    Changed in mien and form and feature—
Scarce the same, that seem'd so lately
    Nature's calmest, gentlest, creature.
Ah, her eye empassion'd flashes
'Neath low-drooping ebon lashes;
And she, listening, stands, unknowing
That the meddling zephyrs blowing
Loose the glittering band, confining
Her rich robe, with gold lace shining;
That her mantle's blown asunder
From her sun-brown'd bosom under,
Heaving with some strange emotion
Like the pulse of summer's ocean.

Tell me why, O high-born Lady!
Dost thou, 'neath yon labyrinth shady
Of acacia, watching, linger,
Parting wide with jewell'd finger

Each intruding twig, corolla?
'Tis for him—for Maspaola!
List! he comes—his arms, his kisses
Seal thy dream's imagined blisses!

To yon arbor, which the fragrant
  Blossoms thickly-mantling cover
(Home of many a crimson vagrant
  Humming-bird), she leads her lover.—
Enter not! ye secret-telling,
For 'tis Love's sequester'd dwelling.

O'er the lake below the City,
  Timely with the oars' soft splashing,
Now is heard some boatman's ditty
  Mingling with their distant dashing;
And the sun, as if regretting
She has vanish'd, now is setting.

A DREAM.

. . . . καὶ τὸ ὕναρ πῇ μὲν ἔκρινεν ἀγαθὸν, ὅτ, ἐνι πόνοις ὢν καὶ κινδύνοις, φῶς μέγα ἐκ Διὸς ἰδεῖν ἔδοξε. . . . . . .

XENOPH. ANAB., B. III. C. I.

I.

At midnight's silent hour I dream'd.
I saw a land with sky o'ercast,
A region aged, dreary, vast,
Where beings lived, or life it seem'd;
Where scarce the orb, that overpass'd
The heavenly way, distinctly beam'd
For faithless mists which ever teem'd,
And light perverted life at last—
So faintly to the mind it gleam'd.

Distress upraised her piteous voice,
And, as the echo on mine ear,

232

I heard a seeming fiend rejoice,
Chilling my startled soul to hear!
I saw a mother sadly weep
Above a tomb but newly made,
And mark'd a maid's pleased fancy keep
Sweet time with flowers her hands essay'd
To twine into a bridal wreath,
But, lo! e'en while she wove the braid,
The flowers were growing sear beneath.
I cast mine eyes where life decay'd,
Saw anxious watchers bending low
O'er one whose breath was thick and slow,
Beheld emotions ebb and flow,
Warm thrills of hope both come and go,
And pallid cheeks o'erflush, and fade—
And turn to hide their voiceless woe!

I heard a joyous peal of laughter
That seem'd as from a purer sphere,
And voices softly sweet to hear;
But, ah, the gloom was darker after—
There, even joy begot a fear.

There were among the medley throng—
Like scattering stars 'tween clouds at night—
Some hearts that beat a silver song,
That winnow'd graces left and right
Around the path they pass'd along,
Leaving behind a radiant light.
Ah me, they were like flowers that bloom
Ere spring in gala-garb is dress'd—
They lived to cheer surrounding gloom:
They lived and died but for the rest.
And, yet, methought that little band,
Within that cloud-enshrouded land,
Was, over all, supremely bless'd.

II.

The dream was changed.—I felt a hand
Of mystic softness seal mine eyes,
And heard a gentle, low command,
As from some viewless distant land:
" Lo, mortal ! follow me—arise."
I floated on, yet knew not where,
Gently as fleecy clouds that flee

Upon the drowsy July air;
I sail'd across a charmed sea.

Soon through the midnight of the way,
An orient vesture met the eye,
Whose ample folds o'erhung the sky
And dazzled like the orb of day.
And suddenly 'twas rent in twain—
The dizzy ken could not behold;
Methought I heard a grand, deep strain
That rapturous grew as on it roll'd,
And, dying, sweeter grew again.
At length return'd the power of sight;
I breathless view'd full many a plain
Whose air seem'd mingling rays of light,
And velvet vale, and verdant lane,
And wood that waved in cool delight,
And, far, a tortuous azure chain
Of mountains of majestic height.

The odorous zephyrs wafted thence,
From nameless, sweet, innumerous flowers,

Intoxication to the sense
As never blooms in earthly bowers.
Slowly I drifted nearer, nearer,
'Neath softer light than solar beams,
And heard wild songsters warbling clearer
'Midst laughter of cool mountain streams.

Delicious grapes o'er dale and hill
Hung ripe in bloomy, purple pride,
And golden fruits, on every side,
Allured the ever-tempted will
With fragrance soft that never died.
Bright peaceful dwellings gleam'd around
'Neath many a vine-clad vocal wood;
And from the flower-enamell'd ground
Uprose a joy-inspiring sound—
The voices of the Wise and Good;
And Beings, in whose beauteous faces
But Love had left ecstatic traces
In smiles that beam'd eternal there,
Were busy with each pleasing care

That makes existence happiness—
Were conning deep, delightful lore,
To whose high mysteries, doom'd to bless,
Earth's mightiest sages cannot soar.

It was a scene of perfect bliss,
A land intense, ethereal, pure,
Where passion ne'er alloy'd a kiss,
Where pleasure ne'er was death's allure.
I heard a voice of soft address,
And saw a smile of vanish'd years;
Received a loved-one's sweet caress—
Awoke, alas! awoke in tears.

21

WRITTEN ON THE HUDSON.

Most lovely Stream! 'tis sweet to flee
From yonder Babylon by the sea,
And, 'mid thy vales and mountains, be
    Awhile at rest,
And, like the wavelets glancing free,
    Float o'er thy breast.

Who can forget when first the eye
Beholds the Catskills, 'gainst the sky,
More beauteous than if they were nigh,
    Far westward stand,
A wall of soft cerulean dye—
    A fairyland?

Yes, River of the Mountains! save
The woods wide-spreading o'er thy wave,

Thy waters, still clear-flowing, lave
    The same sweet scene,
As when the Half-Moon plow'd thy pave
    Of tremulous sheen.

But, now, no Indian's bark canoe
Darts swiftly in and out of view—
Quick as a midnight meteor—through
    Depending vines,
As then to hail old Hudson's crew
    With friendly signs.

Now e'en the Dutch, that dwelt of yore
Upon thy fair, romantic shore,
Live only in thy legend-lore
    And ballad rhyme;
O'er great and small thus triumphs hoar
    Relentless Time.

Methinks, within a bark that sails
Howe'er the current's force prevails—
Like mine that drifts with summer's gales,—

         I can full well
See Irving dreaming those old tales
         He loved to tell.

But he is dead:—as drowsy seems
Quaint Sleepy Hollow, lapp'd in dreams,
And with its wonted beauty teems,
         Though gently wave
The grass and flowers, 'neath summer beams,
         Upon his grave.

And Drake and Halleck—they who sung,
Fair Stream, thy lovely scenes among,
Have pass'd away;—one died when young,
         One linger'd late
To sing (his lyre with cypress hung)
         The other's fate.

But, River! thou dost roll as clear
Whate'er be man's short sad career;
Though Arnold, crush'd by guilt and fear,
         A traitor's name,

Shoved off for life from yonder pier,—
　　Thou art the same.

Thus, e'en though myriad ills have won
Dominion o'er earth's gifted son,
Th' eternal springs of Nature run
　　Full evermore;
'Tis sad—'tis strange,—a mystery none
　　May here explore.

The Highlands cast a deeper eve;
Ha! mark old Crownest's brow receive
A crown, the setting sunbeams weave
　　Of golden light,
Ere o'er the darkening earth they leave
　　The gloom of night.

June, 1876.

THE ANGEL OF SONG.

A Spirit daily comes to me
  With whisper'd songs of heavenly sweetness;
Her home is far beyond a sea
  Where bliss abides in true completeness.

I know not why my Angel-Love
  Delights thus oft to hover round me,
Nor why, from amaranth-vales above,
  To this dark world she came and found me.

At night, when sad I sink to rest,
  With words enwoven in Lydian measure
She twines her arms about my breast—
  Singing me songs of 'wildering pleasure;

And when the morn with queenly grace
  Smiles radiant o'er heaven's azure ocean,
Full oft I feel her light embrace
  And sweet breath breathing warm emotion,

And hear her song, so lulling low,
  And soft-toned lute with cadence holy;
Oh, then hot tears would rise and flow
  That she's of heaven—I earthly, lowly!

At summer eve, when lone I stray
  Afar where Nature slumbers stilly,
While Dian floods a mimic day
  O'er sedgy lake and drowsy lily;

And, when, through watches of the night,
  Dreaming o'er many a glowing ember,
I list the snow-god's hoarse delight
  Weaving the shroud of pale December;—

I hear her robe's soft rustle near;
  Enchantment lends me mystic vision;

Strange music falls upon my ear
　　That spirits hymn in bowers Elysian.

And though she culls immortal flowers
　　In her far-distant happy Thule,
And with their sweets, for hours and hours,
　　Dispels my gloom and loves me truly;

I feel the dank of sordid dust,
　　Nor may I wear a wreath of gladness;
Thus, aye, I mar seraphic trust,
　　And for her smile repay her sadness.

But still she comes with sandal'd feet
　　And golden locks ambrosia-laden;
And still my heart forgets to beat—
　　Loving that more than mortal maiden!

I oft essay to string the shell
　　And breathe her lowliest songs to others;
But, ah! she sings like Israfil
　　Unpeer'd for sweetness 'mong his brothers:

'Tis ever vain,—I fail and weep;

   Earth triumphs over high endeavor.

'Tis my mysterious doom to keep

   A light from heaven—reveal it never.

NIGHT.

Calm Night! thy pall-like vesture falls
  In solemn grandeur o'er the world.
  Beneath thy sombrous shrouds unfurl'd,
Thy dim and awful majesty appalls;
  For, o'er all Nature, broods sublime
A sense as of o'ershadowing doom—
  A semblance of the end, the death of time,
Decaying worlds, quick-fading suns, and nether
  gloom.

Let those who cannot rapture feel
  Ne'er stray with me at midnight-hour:
Awake them not—their souls no rays reveal
Of those deep-kindling fires that steal
Upon my heart, e'en as I kneel
  To some impending, nameless Power!

Night! on thy muffled car swift-driven,
Thou art sublime past mid-day's blazing sun.
If moon-lit, calm,—if lightning-riven,
    When blackening tempests wildly rave on
        high,—
If stars emboss the vault of heaven
    (Thy glittering crown across the sky),—
Thou art, O darksome Queen! in grandeur ever
    one.

SONGS AND BALLADS.

22   249

THISTLE-SEEDS.

A HAPPY child at play,
I blew the thistle's downy seeds,
  And watch'd them lightly float away
Amid the blue autumnal sky,—
    How dear are childish deeds!—
Laugh'd to see them sailing high,
    My winged fairy steeds.

But, now, all sear and dry,
The early flowers of Hope are dead;
  And, while they lowly trampled lie
By stern Misfortune, ruthless Care,
    I take them up instead,
And cast them on the wintry air,
    And sigh—that they are fled!

LITTLE NELL, THE PRIDE OF THE SCHOOL.

A BALLAD.

One January eve, o'er the prairie deserted,
   Little Nell started homeward from school;
With a belt of black clouds the horizon was skirted,
   And the winds sadly moan'd like a ghoul.

As graceful was she as the fawn's every motion;
   The pride of the school was sweet Nell.
The scholars remember her still with devotion,—
   "She was best in her classes," they tell.

Her innocent laugh it was clear as the gushing
   Of hurrying silvery streams,
And softer the glow of her cheek than the blushing
   Of the sky in the summer-eve's beams.

That evening, like waves of a swift, turbid river,
   Soon the clouds fill'd the heavens amain;
Through the crisp wither'd grass, oft a terror-like shiver
   Pass'd fitfully over the plain.

And suddenly snow-flakes—a torrent descending—
   Dash'd round with the blast in its wrath;
Continuously falling and whirling and blending,
   How quickly they cover'd the path!

Alas, how the tempest relentlessly pelted!—
   Little Nell hurried on in despair.
The snow on her cheeks in big teardrops had melted,
   And it hung in the gold of her hair.

Bewilder'd she pray'd for the mercy of Heaven—
   She knew not the way she should go;
But the pitiless flakes were unceasingly driven:
   "Oh God! I am lost in the snow!"

In the darkness, wherever the piercing winds drove
　　her,
　She struggled along through the storm ;
The terrible anguish of freezing was over,
　For numbness had deaden'd her form.

She, staggering, mutter'd,—" Ah me, I am weary."
　In a snow-drift she lay down to rest.
She forgot that the prairie was stormy and dreary ;
　She felt not the snow on her breast.

She was home in the cottage ;—without was the
　　sighing
　Of winds ;—she was warm in her bed.
Alas! 'twas a dream,—the delirium of dying:
　The winds sung a dirge for the dead !

Her parents they sought her afar on the prairie
　Through the snow-storm confusing and blurr'd ;
" NELL !" " NELL !"—ah, how often they shouted ;
　　but ne'er a
　Reply to their calling they heard.

Till the night and the tempest together departed,
    They waited in dreadful suspense,
Hoping fondly, perchance little Nell had not
  started
    When the clouds roll'd so threatening and
    dense.

But at morning they found her asleep, as if
  dreaming,
    Where fatigued she had sunk in the night;
Her long yellow curls they were fluttering and
  gleaming
    O'er her brow, ah! how lifeless and white!

And, weeping, they made her a bed on the
  morrow
    'Neath the snow which would melt and
    depart;
But the weight of the father's and mother's deep
  sorrow—
    Would *that* ever melt from the heart?

Nevermore did her playmates lead Nell to the
    wildwood,
  When in June it is shadowy and cool,
To weave a sweet wreath, in the rapture of child-
    hood,
  And crown her the Pride of the School.

ON THE RECOVERY

OF A PROUD YET BEAUTIFUL YOUNG LADY.

SOMETIMES, O Death, thy stony heart
　　Is soften'd ere thy dart be driven,
And, for a space, thou dost depart
　　To single one more *fit* for heaven.

And, thus, to-day—as those forbear
　　Who mow the vale where lilies grow—
'Mong weeds, there grew a blossom fair;
　　Thy hands forbore to lay it low!—

The daintiest lily in the dell;
　　A queenly bud without a peer.
Ah, Death! thy scythe in pity fell,
　　For one so *proud* should linger here.

"I THINK AYE OF THEE."

PARAPHRASED FROM THE GERMAN OF FRIED-RICH MATTHISSON.

I THINK aye of thee
When the woods, with the glee
Of the nightingales' singing,
Are melodiously ringing.
When think'st thou of me?

I ponder on thee,
As the glimmerings I see
Of the daylight half-faded,
By the fountain o'ershaded.
Where think'st thou of me?

I am dreaming of thee
With sweet anguish,—a sea
Of vague longings appalling;—
Hot tear-drops are falling!—
Dost thou *thus* think of me?

O think thou of me
Till our meeting shall be
In a world not to sever!
Far-distant however,
I dream but of *thee!*

A PICTURE.

I.

THE LADY'S LAMENT.

My silks are the fairest
　At revel and ball,
My gems are the rarest—
　Outflashing them all;
And, yet, though in seeming
　With happiness bless'd,
I'm longing and dreaming—
　Ah! never at rest.

Full many are kneeling
　Imploring my hand,
Their true love revealing—
　For riches and land!

'Twere better though lowly,
  Yea, poverty sweet,
If life were not *wholly*
  A hollow deceit.

My choice never should be
  Of diamond and pearl;
Ah, me! that I could be
  A cottager's girl.—
With purity's blessing,
  How happy to be
One's love, whose caressing
  Were *truly* for me!

II.

THE GIPSY'S LAMENT.

Unknown though at meeting,
  Though loveless to me,
My heart's ever beating,
  Fair Lady, for thee;

Yet, silent and lonely,
　　I scarcely betray
While loving thee only
　　Hope's bitter decay.

In birthright above me
　　A Lady thou art;
Thou never couldst love me
　　Though gentle of heart!
Perchance thou deplorest
　　A sorrow like mine,—
The one thou adorest
　　May never be thine.

Thus fate doth bereave us
　　Of that which is dear,
And pleasure deceive us
　　And be but a tear.
Ah! Lady of beauty,
　　Unloving to me,
My heart is in duty
　　A vassal to thee!

III.

CONCLUSION.

It seems there is given
    With each cup of life
A spell that has driven
    Our reason to strife;
We heed not the measure
    Of weal we possess,
But seek some new pleasure
    We fancy would bless.

Thus life is forever
    A battle in vain,—
To always endeavor,
    Yet never attain:
We waywardly borrow,
    Or lofty or low,
Some balm for our sorrow
    We never shall know!

Alas! as we ponder,
  Whate'er be our share,
We sorrowing wander
  A valley of care;
For we know happiest hours
  Are heralds of pain,
And pleasure's sweet flowers
  Soon wither again.

HOPE.

Ah, Hope! thou bright delusive fire
    Thou sun of our immortal part,
'Tis dreadful when thy beams expire
    Leaving the midnight of the heart.

But thou to man art aye so dear,
    He seldom deems thee all untrue;—
Through disappointment's bitter tear
    He welcomes back thy light anew!

And, thus, I never quite receive
    Conviction thou art false to me,
And fondly, vainly still believe—
    Turning, sweet siren, back to thee.

THE EVENING PAPER;

AN INCIDENT OF THE LATE REBELLION.

———

For the evening paper waiting
　　Eustaleen stood at the gate,
Leaning 'gainst the wicker grating,
　　For the carrier linger'd late.

Though 'twas May—the time of gladness—
　　In her face so paly fair
Was a shade of pensive sadness,
　　That a year had brooded there;

For her lover died, while leading,
　　By a Southern foeman's hand,
On the Rappahannock,—bleeding
　　To preserve his native Land.

266

When commanded to retire
  (His remaining comrades said),
They beheld him fall—expire;
  Thus she knew that he was dead.

And it was for him, who perish'd
  Nobly warring with the foe,
That sweet Eustaleen still cherish'd
  Love and long-enduring woe.

She, for sake of him departed,
  Read at eve the paper still—
How the soldiers, gallant-hearted,
  Conquer'd with as brave a will,—

Weeping for the wives and mothers
  And for *her* that loves as *well*,
When she read the list of others
  Who in each fierce battle fell.

While the robins, newly-mated,
  Sung of love's delicious strength,
Sorrowing Eustaleen awaited
  For the post—which came at length.

'Twas the carrier's voice when speaking
Made her look up in his face;—
Ere a breath, she, faintly shrieking,
Swoon'd within her love's embrace!

Yes! her lover—as arisen
From the tomb to earth above—
From the dreadful Libby prison
Had escaped to life and love!

Often through the summer weather,
Then, those *wedded* lovers read
Of the brave, and wept together
For the prisoners and the dead.

SONG.

Cease to ring, O distant bell—
　　Lovely sound across the lea,
Barely heard o'er hill and dell,—
　　Hush, sweet spirit! flee;
There's a voice that breathes a spell
　　Sweeter far to me.

Beauty—who but feels thy power,
　　Heaven's own essence everywhere?
Stellar sphere and scented flower,
　　Earth and cloud and air,
All possess thy glorious dower;
　　Yet there's *one* most fair.

Sleep, O mere! O gleamy lake,
    With thy moon-lit, silver hue;
Summer wind, O cease to break
    Ripples bright and new;—
There are eloquent eyes that take
    All my love from you!

MAID OF THE MOHAWK.

I.

Fair Maid! like this meandering river,
Thou dost the witching spell possess
To which the heart is vassal ever—
The charm of rustic loveliness;
And like this river, clear and purling,
Thy heart is pure, unknown to guile;
From 'neath thine auburn tresses curling,
Methinks thou couldst but only smile!

II.

I've seen full many a pastoral valley,
But none like this delightful scene
With emerald dell, and forest alley
Whose boughs the sunbeams dance between;

Yet, thou, with lea and wood agreeing,
Though fairer than Arcadian dale,
Dost seem their Nymph, in beauty being
Well suited to so sweet a vale.

III.

The world to me is often dreary
Where hearts become so hard and cold,
Till, sick of show, I grow how weary
Of those who bow them down to gold,
And almost hate the sullen bustle
Of men who care for naught beside,
And turn me from the silken rustle
Of Beauty pale, in pamper'd pride;

IV.

But, Maiden, thou canst not dissemble—
Unskill'd in falsehood's worldly ways;
Ah, how thine eyes' long lashes tremble
And droop at but a word of praise!

Ah me, if all the earth were only
  Composed of spirits such as thou,
'Twould be a heaven—and never lonely,
  And sad, and dark, and drear, as now!

V.

I love the voice that hails the flowers
  Of bosky shade and sunny glade,
That learns their names in leisure hours
  And makes them friends before they fade,—
That carols oft, 'mid breath of clover,
  Sweet ballads in the fields afar,
When twilight glimmers, toil is over,
  And golden is the evening star.

VI.

I love the mind that sees the glory
  In Nature's face, which ne'er expires,
That loves the forest, gnarl'd and hoary,
  Whose leaves are wild æolian lyres,—

·The soul that scorns the paltry pleasure
  Of those who kneel at Fashion's shrine,
Yet quaffs the drainless, mantling measure
  Of all creation's nectarous wine.

VII.

I love the hand whose taper fingers
  Are stain'd with strawberries growing wild,
And graceful foot whose small print lingers
  Impress'd amidst the violets mild,
And peachy cheek where health's reflected,
  By summer suns kiss'd darkly fair,
And hair thrown back as if neglected
  In ringlets on the caressing air.

VIII.

And such art thou, O Mohawk Maiden!
  Wild floweret of this sweet retreat.—
'Tis sad the loveliest blossoms fade in
  The sun's unclouded light and heat;

Thy soft dark eyes, that smile in duty,
   Thy nut-brown cheeks, thy tresses curl'd,
Thy vermeil lips, would lose their beauty
   Amidst the heartless busy world.

IX.

Below yon hills so gently swelling,
   The murmuring Mohawk at my feet,
To lodge in some sequester'd dwelling
   In thy calm vale were truly sweet;
Ah, yes, my heart could dwell forever
   Most happy here with bliss and thee,
Remembering care and sorrow never;—
   Thy soul would mirror heaven to me.

X.

But, no.—My thoughts full oft are lowly,
   Nor could exalt me to the peer
Of one, like thee, so chaste and holy;
   I'll on—and leave thee joyous here!

And, yet, sweet Maid, I'll ne'er forget thee,
    Nor this lone spot of peace and rest;
Thine innocence, here where I met thee,
    Shall keep thee happy, make thee bless'd!

HERKIMER CO., NEW YORK, June, 1876.

"AH, NOW THE SONG IS FLOWN."

I.

Ah, now the song is flown,
   And bliss and day have fled,
For I am here alone ;—
Her presence fill'd the night
With more than heavenly light,
   But now the day is dead.

II.

I strove to prove my heart
   It never could be so ;
For something seems to start
So vaguely back on me,—
Prophetic, it may be,
   Of tears and future woe.

SIR TRISTRAM'S SONG TO QUEEN ISOUDE.

I.

When the dim daylight is fading,
   Homeward is hieing the bee
While the spiced meadowland's lading
   Balm on the air of the lea,
Beneath dark mountains o'ershading
   Grander at dusk seem to be;
Isoude! 'tis blissful, my fair,
   Sweet beyond earthly degree,
Out in the soft evening air
   Only, yes, only with thee!

II.

Oft, when the world, stilly dreaming,
   Wrapp'd in the mantle of Night,

Sees not the stars that are beaming
    Numberless, glorious, and bright,
Feels not elate from the gleaming
    Moon and her tremulous light;
Darling! thy smile to me seems
    Blent with the beautiful sight,
Filling my heart with its beams,
    Waking a purer delight.

III.

Come while the breath of the clover
    Floats from the sweet sunny dell;
Come, while the forest-trees over
    Sound their æolian shell;
Lead me, O loveliest rover!
    Charm'd by thy magical spell,
Where thou art wont to repair,—
    Lead where the wild-flowers dwell,
Lilies that cannot compare
    With the white hands that impel.

. IV.

Bitter howe'er be the hour,
   All is delight when we meet;
Life, with its sunshine and shower,
   Lost in the tread of thy feet,
In the soft step that the flower
   Rises from under complete,—
Lost in thy presence, thy charms,
   In the heart's flutter and beat—
Kisses—entwining of arms—
   Almost with heaven replete!

A LOVER'S LOVE-BALLAD.

Dear Molly, you're sweet, and you know it,—
  Your lips seem to pout for a kiss;
You're pretty—and like well to show it!
  You were *fair* if it were not for *this*.

The fact is, my dear, you're too saucy—
  You think you're the empress of beaux!
You fancy your tresses, so glossy,
  Were made to enchain them like foes.

But you know just as well as I tell you
  (Now, please don't begin to say nay!)
You, at times, can *endure* a beau;—well, you
  Are a woman,—she fails in this way.—

For convenience, you little deceiver,
  You wore me around like a glove;
I was troubled sometimes with a fever
  And headache,—it might have been love:

But your vows are now hopelessly broken,—
  There's Jenkens he calls you his dear:
Alas! my poor heart is not oaken;
  Ah me, I'm dissolved in a tear!

But, Molly, I think I'm not *dying;*—
  There'll ne'er be a lack of sweet girls
So artlessly, innocently trying
  To entangle a beau in their curls.

Now, Molly, my sweetest, *please won't you?*
  You know you were made to be kiss'd;
Good-by, then, my darling,— O, don't you
  Imagine this once will be miss'd!

SONNETS.

ON A DESERTED COTTAGE

IN THE ALLEGHANY MOUNTAINS.

Go on.—Here let me linger for a space.
  Ah me, yon cottage in this mountain dell
  Was once more homelike; busy footsteps fell
  Upon its floors.   Past time steals back apace;
And, by yon fireside, smile a father's face,
  A mother's, son's, and daughter's;—who could
      tell
  How beauteous is this maid?   The very spell
  Of this wild scene, the mountain streamlet's
      grace,
Are in her eyes and motions!   Blessed spot—
  Peace, beauty, love, and innocence are there.

25   285

Hark, happy laughter rings within the cot:
A girlish voice now hums a merry air.
    Alas! I dream; or dead or far away
    Are all those hearts—the cottage in decay.

ON THE DEATH OF ADA.

Ada, shall I behold thee nevermore?
  Art thou, indeed, to Death forever wed?
  Sometimes I scarce believe thy spirit fled:—
  Forgetful, oft, I linger at the door
To hear thee sweetly singing, as of yore,
  Then dreadful is the truth—that thou art dead!
  Philosophy the bitter tears I shed
  Cannot assuage with all its vaunted lore—
Vain comforter! that mocks the couch of death.
  Were't mine to die, I would not fate bewail;
  But, oh, what consolation can avail
When thou art in the grave bereft of breath?
  Alas! the end of earthly love—to know
  The crushing weight of unavailing woe!

ON READING SHELLEY.

The poet true need doubt not his reward.
　To him is given the gift of second sight;
　He half-perceives the presence of the bright
　Invisible angels; wondrously accord
His thoughts with Nature; he becomes the ward
　Of heavenly Beauty, whose inspiring light
　Dwells in him, though he wanders in the night
　Of sorrow; he is Nature's truest lord.
When those who dwell around him all have pass'd
　From life to death, and ravenous decay
　Has wasted all their petty works and cast
Oblivion endless o'er their names,—his lay
　Shall live in many a heart unto the last,
　His memory growing greener day by day.

288

ADIEU TO LIFE.

WHEN, SEVERELY WOUNDED, I WAS LYING IN
A FOREST, HELPLESS AND IN EXPECTATION
OF DEATH.

FROM THE GERMAN OF KÖRNER.

My pale lips quiver;—how my wound doth burn!
 By my spent heart, now fluttering faint and low,
 I feel my life is ended here below.
 God! 'tis thy will;—resign'd to Thee I turn.
What golden prospects I did aye discern—
 The beauteous dreams change to a dirge of woe.
 Courage!—There dwells within my heart, I
  know,
 That which shall deathless live beyond that
  bourne,

With all that was so sacred here to me,
     For which I burn'd with restless, youthful fire,
     Whether I call'd it love or liberty!
But, lo, above me bends an angel bright;—
     Soft airs—as now my senses slow expire—
     Upbear me to th' aurora-tinted height!

TO —— ——.

—

Though well I know the West is not a land
  Where one may prosper by poetic lore—
  For here mankind, to Mammon given o'er,
  But worship gold, and toil with greedy hand,
Nor know that by each zephyr soft are fann'd
  Bright Muses' tresses, beauteous as of yore,—
  Yet, I shall cull sweet roses, as before,
  Content to scorn the mercenary band.—
What, did I say that none, here, love the song
  Of Shakspeare and the rest?—O, no! for thou
  Dost feel their power; thou dost perceive the
      birth
And death of beauty in the world—dost long
  To quaff th' ideal nectarous. Haply, now,
  Thou feel'st what Mammon cannot feel on earth.

ON A FAVORITE CAT NAMED DON JUAN.

"Don Juan was a bachelor of arts,
   And parts, and hearts,"—I think, thus sings the
      poet;
   And as for my cat Juan, you would know it
   E'en at a glance—to see his pranks and starts,
As round my legs and o'er my lap he darts,
   Proud of the very ways he has to show it!
   Whate'er a studious cat can master, lo, it
   Is known to him—a lad of brilliant parts:
And, when he hies him forth at close of day
   To bask him in his lady's loving eye,
   And round about with all their friends they stray
Carousing over fence and housetop high,
   Their nightly revelry reminds me truly
   Of amorous Juan and his Donna Julia.

NOTES.

293

NOTES.

PAGE 17.

Within a sombre, wild fiord
The Viking built a dragon fleet.

The Norsemen called their barks Dragons and Serpents, perhaps because they were embellished with rude carvings representing dragons and other monsters.—V. Michelet's "France," b. ii. ch. iii.

PAGE 19.

The giants dire that lived of yore,
That, turn'd to stone, through murky sky
Scowl downward with the look they wore.

"We have just passed the Arctic circle, at a singular island, rising in the form of a giant horseman from the waters. The back of his mantle is the mountain-side, and the crags and cliffs make the horse's head and ears, and the rider's hand. His head was at first veiled angrily in mist;

but as we passed, a whiff carried it away, and a grand, calm face, like the face of the Sphinx, stood out, looking solemnly up to the stormy sky. The effect was mysterious and wonderful. . . . . . . One can imagine how many a fisher-boat's crew has watched anxiously and superstitiously the head of the giant rider, and, though Christian, has muttered a prayer against Jumala or the Trolls."—BRACE'S " Norse-Folk," p. 67.

PAGE 33.

> . . . . *ah, why forsake*
> *The Norse, the fittest for the sea?*

It is said that the old Norse had one hundred and fifty words to signify the *sea* in its different aspects.

PAGE 84.

> . . . . *these and the thousand*
> *All-nameless charms that, intermingling, blend,*
> *Forming the whole, are all how beautiful—*
> *How beautiful!*

> " Beautiful !
> How beautiful is all this visible world !"

> " Manfred," Act I. Scene II.

PAGE 112.

The thousand voices that from every brake, etc.

" Es dringen die Blüthen

Aus jedem Zweig,

Und tausend Stimmen

Aus dem Gesträuch."—GOETHE.

PAGE 113.

While o'er their heads the maple's tasselly blooms
Crimson the twigs.

The maple here referred to (*Acer rubrum*) is commonly
known as the red or swamp maple. The flowers of this
species are mostly scarlet or crimson, while the flowers of
the other maples are generally greenish or of a pale or
greenish yellow.

PAGE 138.

Far had they come from where the wave
Of clear Scioto, gently flowing, etc.

At the time the incidents related in this poem are supposed
to have occurred, the Shawnees lived on the Scioto River.
The distance between the scene of the tale—the Moxahala
—and the Scioto, was considered by both the wandering

Indian and the tireless backwoodsman as but a moderate ramble of a few days.

PAGE 140.

Ye braves! when he,

My Father, yon bright Sun, etc.

This thought and that in the seventeenth line below, are taken from the words of the heroic Tecumseh, who was, in later times, the Chief of the Shawnees. It was at a council held at Vincennes, in 1810, by General Harrison when governor of the Northwest Territory; the object of the council was to insure peace between the Shawnees and the territorial government. Tecumseh made his appearance at the appointed time; and General Harrison, as governor, invited him to come forward and take a seat by his side, saying that it was the wish of *their* "Great Father," the President of the United States, that he should do so. On hearing this, Tecumseh stretched himself to his greatest height, and, looking haughtily around over the throng assembled at the council, said in tones that could be distinctly heard to its farthest extremities: "*My* Father?—The Sun is *my* Father and the Earth is my mother—and on her bosom I will recline." He and his warriors immediately stretched themselves on the green grass. It is said the

effect was wonderful; for some moments there was profound silence. The above may be found related at length
in BARBER's " History of the Western States," pp. 160 and
161, where it is cited from LAW's "Colonial History of
Post Vincennes."

PAGE 153.

. . . . . . thou mak'st to roll

The suns and worlds through heaven, etc.

This is an allusion to the last line of *La Divina Com-
media :*

" L'amor che muove 'l Sole e l'altre stelle."

PAGE 167.

But, suddenly, howl and horrid yell, etc.

In the year 1763, Pontiac, a chief of the Ottawas, who
had been an ally of the French, secretly formed a great
confederation of the Algonquin tribes to exterminate the
English west of the Alleghany mountains. The tribes that
united in this memorable struggle were the Shawnees, Ottawas, Miamies, Chippewas, Wyandots, Pottawatomies,
Mississaguies, Ontagamies, Winnebagoes, and Senecas.
So artfully had Pontiac matured his plans, that, until the

first blow was struck in June, none of the commanders of the western forts had the least suspicion of the impending danger. During the summer he captured all the posts west of Oswego, New York, except Detroit, Fort Pitt, and Niagara. Thus, through the greater part of summer and the following autumn, the whole of the Northwest was exposed to the ravages of the Indians; and they failed not to take advantage of the opportunity. The massacre, and the burning of the cabin on the shore of Lake Seneca, New York, are supposed to have happened in the fall of that year. See LOSSING's "History of the United States," part iv. ch. xii., etc.

PAGE 185.

Ah, yes! give me the rustic cot,
The meadow, wold, and garden plot,—
The glory of a lowly lot,
　　　Where Peace may come and build her nest!

Although the passage is so well known, I cannot forbear quoting, in connection with the above lines, a paragraph from a letter of Mr. Murdoch to Joseph Cooper Walker, describing the house in which the poet Burns was born. Speaking of the father of the poet, he says: " In this parish [Alloway], on the roadside, a Scotch mile and a half from the town of Ayr, and half a mile from the bridge of Doon, William Burnes took a piece of land, consisting of about seven acres; part of which he laid out in garden ground, and part of which he kept to graze a cow, etc., still continuing in the employ of Provost Ferguson. Upon this little farm was erected a humble dwelling, of which William Burnes was the architect. It was, with the exception of a little straw, literally a tabernacle of clay. In this mean cottage, of which I myself was at times an inhabitant, I really believe there dwelt a larger portion of content than in any palace in Europe. The 'Cotter's Saturday Night' will give some idea of the temper and manners that prevailed there."

PAGE 195.

O how sweet were a Lethean measure
To deaden the memory of Pleasure
When the bright-tinted bubble is burst!

This sentiment is ever new, yet it was old when Dante wrote the oft-quoted lines:

. . . . . . "nessun maggior dolore,
Che ricordarsi del tempo felice
Nella miseria. . . . . . ."

PAGE 227.

Watching many an island, slowly
    Floating 'neath th' o'ershadowing mountains
    O'er the lake, etc.

At the time of the conquest by Cortés, the lakes in the valley of Anahuac were covered with floating-islands, bearing their rich freight of fruits and flowers and drifting "like enchanted isles over the waters." Describing the march of the Spaniards to the City of Mexico, Prescott says: "They were amazed, also, by the sight of the chinampas, or floating-gardens,—those wandering islands of verdure, to which we shall have occasion to return hereafter,—teeming with flowers and vegetables, and moving like rafts over the waters." And again exclaims the same beautiful writer: "How gay and picturesque must have been the aspect of the lake [Tezcuco] in those days, with its shining cities, and flowering islets rocking, as it were, at anchor on the fair bosom of its waters!"

Though the wall of mountains surrounding the valley of Anahuac is leagues distant from the City of Mexico, yet, through the clear atmosphere of that elevated plateau the mountains seemed to the Aztecs very near, looming over the orchards, maize-fields, and lakes below.

PAGE 228.

While her fingers idly braided
Garlands sweet of flowers unfaded.

The love of flowers was universal among the Aztecs. They used them in their religious ceremonies, and cultivated them in beautiful and extensive gardens when, in Europe, their cultivation was almost unknown. Their flat house-tops were often so arranged as to appear a tangled profusion of flowers of all colors, rivalling in beauty the hanging-gardens of Babylon. See PRESCOTT's " Conquest of Mexico."

THE END.

www.ingramcontent.com/pod-product-compliance
Lightning Source LLC
Chambersburg PA
CBHW020937120726
47905CB00008B/2564